D0044430

My name is Barry Allen, and I'm the fastest man alive.

A particle accelerator explosion sent a bolt of lightning into my lab one night, shattering a shelf of containers and dousing me in electricity and chemicals. When I woke up from a coma nine months later, I found I was gifted with superspeed.

Since then, I've worked to keep Central City and its people safe from those with evil intent. With the help of my friends Caitlin and Cisco at S.T.A.R. Labs; my girlfriend, Iris; her brother, Wally; and my adoptive father, Joe, I've battled time travelers, mutated freaks, and metahumans of every stripe.

I've tried to reconcile my past, learned some tough lessons, and—most important of all—never, ever stopped moving forward.

I am . . .

THE FLASH

BY BARRY LYGA

FLASH™

THE TORNADO TWINS

AMULET BOOKS

NEW YORK

To Paul Levitz and Keith Giffen. They didn't invent the future, but they sure gave it an upgrade!

PUBLISHER'S NOTE: This is a work of fiction. Names, characters, places, and incidents are either the product of the author's imagination or used fictiously, and any resemblance to actual persons, living or dead, business establishments, events, or locales is entirely coincidental.

Cataloging-in-Publication Data has been applied for and may be obtained from the Library of Congress.

ISBN 978-1-4197-3124-2

ABBO40251

Cover illustration by César Moreno
Book design by Chad W. Beckerman

Printed and bound in U.S.A.
10 9 8 7 6 5 4 3 2 1

Amulet Books are available at special discounts when purchased in quantity for premiums and promotions as well as fundraising or educational use. Special editions can also be created to specification. For details, contact specialsales@abramsbooks.com or the address below.

ABRAMS The Art of Books
195 Broadway, New York, NY 10007
abramsbooks.com

PREVIOUSLY IN

THE FLASH

As Barry Allen knows well, no matter how fast you are, you can't outrun your problems.

First, a techno-wizard named Hocus Pocus came to Central City and made the Flash his plaything. After some hard work, fast feet, and quick thinking, Barry and his friends were able to trick the villain at his own game. Things were almost back to normal, until Hocus Pocus vanished from a secure cell in the Pipeline.

Desperate to figure out Hocus Pocus's insanely advanced technology, Barry set out for Earth 2 and some help from Harrison Wells. But his trip went awry, and he ended up on Earth 27, where all the people he knew as heroes back home were villains, and vice versa. With the help of the Rogues (who were good guys on Earth 27) and the mysterious Madame Xanadu, Barry defeated the evil speedster Johnny Quick and returned to Earth 1. He didn't come home empty-handed, either; he gained the knowledge of Johnny Quick's "speed mantra," which unlocked a direct connection to HyperHeaven and made Barry faster than ever before.

Now he's going to need that speed! Back on Earth 1, Earthworm continues his killing spree in the sewers. While Barry was away, Kid Flash headed down there to stop him. He was ambushed and now is trapped in the dark, helpless as hundreds of rats converge on him. And Barry's job at CCPD hangs by a thread. On top of all that, Cisco has vibed an eerie truth about Hocus Pocus: He's from the future. Really, really far in the future. Like, thousands of years in the future.

And Barry is determined to go get him . . .

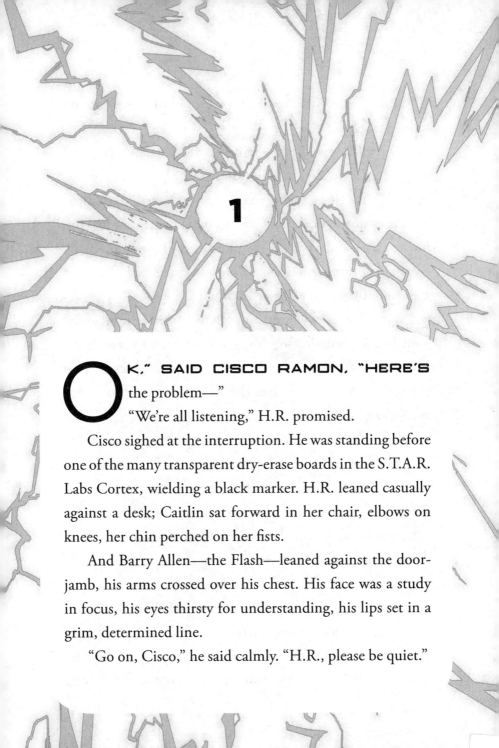

1

OK," SAID CISCO RAMON, "HERE'S the problem—"

"We're all listening," H.R. promised.

Cisco sighed at the interruption. He was standing before one of the many transparent dry-erase boards in the S.T.A.R. Labs Cortex, wielding a black marker. H.R. leaned casually against a desk; Caitlin sat forward in her chair, elbows on knees, her chin perched on her fists.

And Barry Allen—the Flash—leaned against the door-jamb, his arms crossed over his chest. His face was a study in focus, his eyes thirsty for understanding, his lips set in a grim, determined line.

"Go on, Cisco," he said calmly. "H.R., please be quiet."

H.R. opened his mouth, then thought better of it and saluted instead.

"We all know about parallel worlds," Cisco said, and he proceeded to draw a series of overlapping circles on the board. "Fifty-two variants of our own universe, all occupying the same physical space but separated by vibrational frequencies. So far, so easy." He paused, as though expecting an interruption, and glanced meaningfully at H.R., who mimed pulling a zipper over his mouth.

With a pleased expression, Cisco continued. He drew a line on the board. "So, this is one universe in the Multiverse. Time flows in one direction—from the present into the future. Again, easy. But there's a theory that says that each universe in the Multiverse contains its own specific variants. That each choice we make in *this* universe splits the timeline, creating alternate versions." He sketched scattered lines branching off from the main line. "Eat pizza for lunch—that's one version of the future. Eat a P, B, and J—that's another one. Most of the variants aren't different enough to matter. You'd never notice the difference—"

"Unless you looked at your napkin," H.R. offered.

Cisco groaned. "You'd *rarely* notice the difference. But in some cases . . . In some cases, there are big enough changes that one version of the future could be unrecognizable as compared to another. Same timeline, same universe, different outcomes."

The board was now a flurry of lines breaking off from the main one. It seemed hopeless.

"Lotta possibilities," Cisco continued. "We need to make sure you find your way through all this mess to the proper future, the *one timeline* that results in the Hocus Pocus who came back in time to challenge you."

More silence. You could almost hear brains churning.

"All water runs to the sea," Barry said into the quiet.

Everyone turned to him. "What was that?" Caitlin asked.

Barry strolled to the board and took a red marker from the cradle. "Pretend the main branch of the timeline is a river. All these breakouts that Cisco drew"—he circled a bunch of them in red—"are what potamologists—people who study rivers, H.R.—call distributaries, where the water flows outside the normal bed. But . . ."

At the mention of the word *distributaries,* Cisco flinched. Barry noticed but said nothing and went on. With a flourish, he began extending the distributaries, adding to them with his red marker, curving them back until they reconnected with the main timeline again, then circling big red loops around the terminus, where all lines intersected.

"For the most part, bodies of water flow from smaller to bigger to biggest. Distributaries eventually become tributaries, which recombine with the main river and flow to the biggest body of water, the sea. Or, in this case, the future."

Cisco shook his head. "Yeah, I've thought of that, but the more I brain it out, the more I'm not so sure we can apply water-table physics to time travel. It works as a metaphor, but does it actually *work*?"

"If you don't like earth sciences, how about simple algebra?" Barry challenged. "It's possible to have multiple, different factors that lead to the same answer. Say x-squared equals four, and you're trying to solve for x."

"Even I know this one!" H.R. chortled. "Two!"

Barry shook his head. "Nope. There are *two* answers: two and negative two. Square either one of them, and you get four."

Cisco was pacing and—quite unconsciously—vibrating just the tiniest bit. Only Barry, with his speed-attuned vision, noticed it. "I'm still not sure," Cisco mumbled. "Algebra and potamology can't match up to quantum weirdness and metaphysics.

"And then there's also the matter of speed," he went on. "The tachyon harness is busted but good, and it's gonna take a long time to fix it. Which means you've got no speed boost. You've broken the time barrier before, but in the *other* direction, going into the past. And even then, only by a day or so.

You're talking about traveling thousands of years and in the other direction. No offense, bro, but I'm not sure you've got the speed."

Barry grinned broadly. "Don't worry about speed. That's not an issue any longer."

Caitlin turned in her chair, raising an eyebrow. "Not that I don't appreciate the confidence, but would you like to share with the rest of the class?"

"Yeah, show us what you've got under the hood, B.A.!" H.R. crowed.

Barry ignored them and considered his friend for a moment. Cisco had always been a bit headstrong and usually concerned about safety. Not to this degree, though. His attitude was almost always, *Let's throw some science at this and do damage control later!* Now, he was being uncharacteristically cautious.

"Is there something I should know?" Barry asked gently.

Cisco cracked his knuckles and seemed suddenly too aware of Caitlin and H.R.'s presence. He sidled up to Barry. "Can we talk? Alone?"

Barry arched an eyebrow. He liked to keep things out in the open. Fewer opportunities for hurt feelings and misunderstandings. But, sure. Cisco had earned a little privacy.

He threw an arm around his buddy's shoulders and guided him out into the hallway.

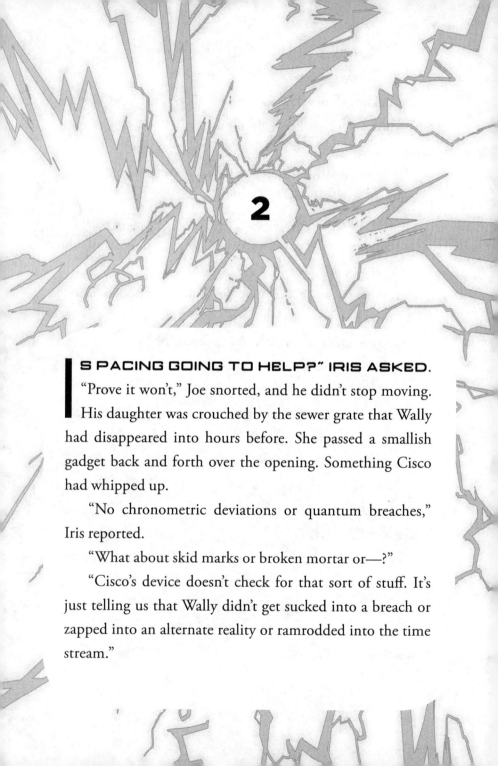

2

IS PACING GOING TO HELP?" IRIS ASKED.

"Prove it won't," Joe snorted, and he didn't stop moving.

His daughter was crouched by the sewer grate that Wally had disappeared into hours before. She passed a smallish gadget back and forth over the opening. Something Cisco had whipped up.

"No chronometric deviations or quantum breaches," Iris reported.

"What about skid marks or broken mortar or—?"

"Cisco's device doesn't check for that sort of stuff. It's just telling us that Wally didn't get sucked into a breach or zapped into an alternate reality or ramrodded into the time stream."

"Yeah," Joe said, his voice laden with sarcasm and parental fear, "because those are the only dangerous things that could possibly—"

Just then, the street beneath them . . .

Vibrated.

Wally shut his eyes tightly. For some reason, it was less scary being trapped in the dark when you were making the darkness yourself. As a child, when he'd been afraid of the dark—the stillness, the occasional hacking cough from his mother dying in another room—he'd squeeze his eyes closed, and the dark became *purposeful*, not something to be feared. It worked again here and now.

Except for the rats.

They raced toward him in the filthy water, their bodies plashing and rippling. Any second now, they would be on him. Cisco's suit would provide some protection, but his face was unprotected, and it was too easy to imagine small, sharp teeth sinking into his flesh, stripping back his cheeks, laying bare his skull . . .

Settle down, West. That's not how a hero goes out. You've faced down some bad nastiness before, and you're not about to shuffle off this mortal coil as rodent chow. No way. No how.

He was still backed up against a wall. *No rats coming from that direction,* he thought. Could rats crawl down walls from above? *Ugh. Don't think about* that. *Focus on what's ahead.*

With both hands in the water, Wally braced himself against the floor and kicked his feet at superspeed. A roar filled the chamber as water thrummed and churned. Anything caught in its path would be knocked down, knocked over, knocked out.

With more and more fury, he kicked. The water rose and crashed, a mini tsunami there in the sewers. The floor and walls around him shook. Sediment filtered down from the ceiling, causing him to cough, but he kept up his speed.

Within moments, the rats had scattered. A few slick, furry bodies brushed past him, but they were harmless now, crushed and broken by the sheer force of the water he'd riled.

Water pressure. Not just a fact but a friend!

He grinned to himself. OK, so the rats were no longer a threat. And the silence in the chamber told him that Earthworm was gone.

Good.

He opened his eyes.

It was still pitch-black.

He was still trapped.

OK, but two out of three ain't bad . . .

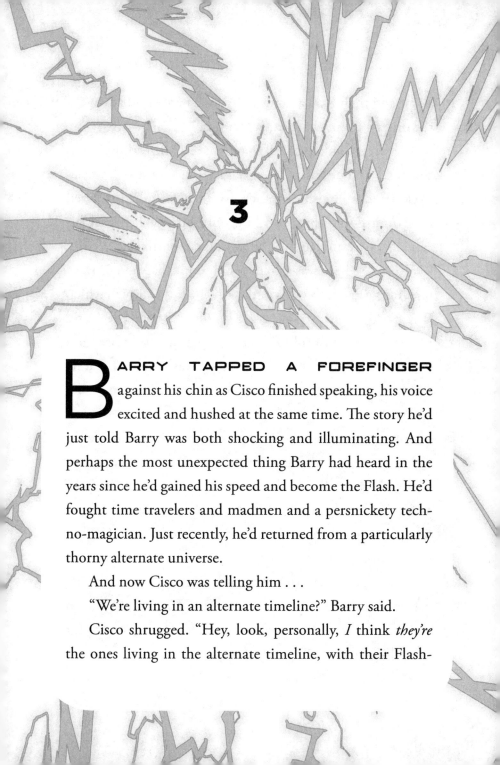

3

BARRY TAPPED A FOREFINGER against his chin as Cisco finished speaking, his voice excited and hushed at the same time. The story he'd just told Barry was both shocking and illuminating. And perhaps the most unexpected thing Barry had heard in the years since he'd gained his speed and become the Flash. He'd fought time travelers and madmen and a persnickety techno-magician. Just recently, he'd returned from a particularly thorny alternate universe.

And now Cisco was telling him . . .

"We're living in an alternate timeline?" Barry said.

Cisco shrugged. "Hey, look, personally, *I* think *they're* the ones living in the alternate timeline, with their Flashpoint and their Savitar and some dude named Julian. We're the original. But whatever. Semantics."

Barry remembered well the night after defeating Zoom, the night he'd decided to go back in time and stop Reverse-Flash from killing his mother. Iris's presence had stopped him from doing that, and he'd only infrequently cast his thoughts back to that possibility in the months since.

But now here was Cisco, telling him that he'd vibed a meeting with *another* Cisco, this one from a reality in which Barry had, in fact, gone back in time, stopped Reverse-Flash . . . and, instead of creating a personal paradise, he'd botched the job, making a reality that was so flawed that he had no choice but to go back in time *again*, this time to let his mother die and set things right.

Only, according to that other Cisco, things *hadn't* gone right. The reset hadn't put the universe back the way it had been originally. Some glitches came through from Flash-point: The villainous "god of speed" called Savitar, a set of dangerous powers and a split personality to boot for Caitlin.

Dante's death . . .

"You see why all this alternate timeline stuff is making me extra nervous, right?" Cisco said. "What if you run to the future but end up stuck in the Flashpoint future? Or something like that?"

"Cisco, I—"

Cisco grabbed Barry and pushed him against the wall. Panic and worry spun in his eyes. "What if you go and *we can't get you back?*"

Barry bristled at Cisco's physicality, but he realized it came from genuine anguish. Cisco wasn't being a bully; he was being a scared friend.

"It'll be OK," he told him. "We'll make it work."

Cisco stepped back, running his hands through his hair over and over again, telegraphing his anxiety. "How can you be so sure we'll figure it out?"

Barry grinned. "Because we always *do*."

With a tight, humorless smile, Cisco shook his head. "I wish I shared your boundless confidence right about now, buddy. We're in uncharted territory here. If you were going a few days or even a few years into the future, I might not be so worried. Heck, if you wanted to jog a mere four hundred years to the twenty-fifty century and beat the snot out of Eobard Thawne when he was a punk kid, I'd probably sign off on that. But we're talking *millennia* into the future. Who knows what kind of quantum weirdness we'd be talking about? So many variables, and now we *know* that alternate timelines are a factor. You could end up in a different where, a different *when*. You could find yourself in a timeline where you're a different *you*."

"Possibly," Barry mused aloud, "but do you know who I've been thinking about this whole time?"

"Rosario Dawson?" Cisco shrugged. "No? Just me? OK, who?"

"Georg Wilhelm Richmann."

"Who?"

"He was a Swedish scientist obsessed with Ben Franklin's experiments with electricity. He decided to duplicate the whole kite-and-string-and-key bit and got smacked in the head with a ball of lightning that ended up killing him."

Cisco nodded slowly. "I'm waiting—patiently, I might add—for the part where the story has a happy ending."

"My point is that this is what we do, Cisco." Barry clapped a firm hand onto Cisco's shoulder. "We risk. We charge in. We challenge the unknown. A couple of years ago, a ball of lightning smacked *me* in the head. Should have killed me. Guess what? Still standing. Sometimes you're Ben; sometimes you're Georg. What follows is what matters."

He beamed broadly at Cisco, who sighed in defeat. "Your endless, ennobling optimism is becoming really annoying. Let's figure out how to get you to the future, you pain in my butt."

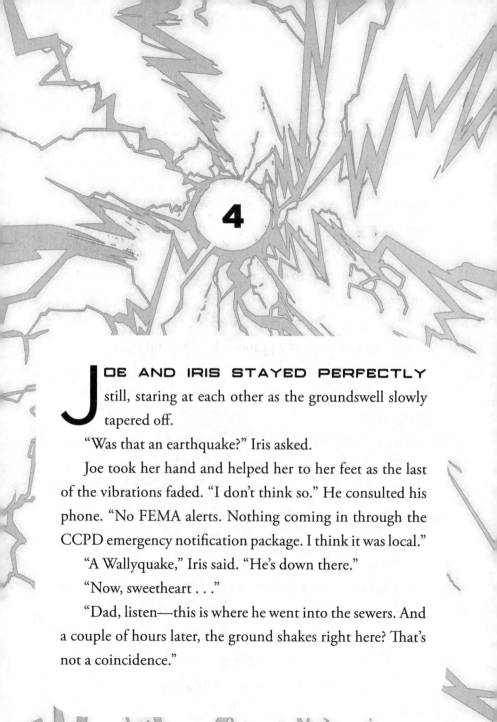

4

JOE AND IRIS STAYED PERFECTLY
still, staring at each other as the groundswell slowly
tapered off.

"Was that an earthquake?" Iris asked.

Joe took her hand and helped her to her feet as the last
of the vibrations faded. "I don't think so." He consulted his
phone. "No FEMA alerts. Nothing coming in through the
CCPD emergency notification package. I think it was local."

"A Wallyquake," Iris said. "He's down there."

"Now, sweetheart . . ."

"Dad, listen—this is where he went into the sewers. And
a couple of hours later, the ground shakes right here? That's
not a coincidence."

"Baby, if he's down there, we have no way of finding him. Those tunnels are like a maze. We need to— What are you doing?"

Iris was leaning against Joe's shoulder, pulling off her shoes. "These cost a month's pay. Worth every penny, but I'm not getting them mucky down there."

Joe recoiled, horrified. "I'm not letting you go down there!"

"You can't stop me," she said sweetly, "unless you plan on arresting me."

"Don't think that hasn't crossed my mind many, many times over the years," he grumbled. "*I'll* go down."

"I'm smaller, Dad. I can fit into places you can't. Don't worry—I won't go far. I'm just looking for clues to where Wally is."

As he helped her navigate the ladder into the close and fetid depths of the sewer, Joe couldn't help thinking: *Of all the stupid things you've done in your life, Joe West, is this the stupidest?*

Not terribly far from where his father and sister were arguing, Wally West lay panting and pleased in the darkness. Yeah, it sucked to be stuck in a sewer, but stuck in a sewer without a million hungry rats was a step in the right direction.

Now he had to figure out how to get out of there. Super-speed was no good in this case: Without light to guide him, he'd go smashing into walls, careening off pipes. His head would be bashed in by his own speed before he made it ten feet. Even if he somehow managed to avoid collisions, he'd still be trapped in a pitch-black maze, running blindly for who knew how long.

Light. Light. He needed *light*, and his phone was busted and lost somewhere in the water.

We had light before electricity, he reminded himself. *It's not as if Caveman Ogg and Cavelady Ooga didn't have romantic candlelight dinners of mastodon steak, right?*

So, fire. In the wet. Without any matches. Easier said than done.

He slumped against the wall and did his very best Barry Allen impression, not that anyone could see it or appreciate it. Wally wasn't stupid, but Barry was a genius, and if anyone could think of a way to square this particular circle, it would be Barry.

At his speed, he could create enough friction to make fire from two pieces of wood rubbed together . . . but there was no wood at hand, no way to find any in the dark, and it would be wet, besides.

OK, so . . . what about stones? Flints were struck against rocks to create sparks. He could get some loose chunks of concrete and maybe hit them together fast enough against the wall to create a spark . . .

Which, again, would have nothing to burn. Because everything down here was wet, wet, wet.

Except . . .

A thought occurred to him. Standing, he unzipped the chest piece of his costume down to the end of his sternum. Inside, the uniform was still dry. Maybe this could act as tinder?

He probed around inside the costume for a seam, somewhere to rip out some fabric. His probing fingers found not a seam but rather a tear, no doubt from one of his spills during his fight with Earthworm. Something fibrous puffed out from the rip. It felt almost like steel wool but extremely fine. Almost soft. Cisco had probably used it to cushion certain tech built into the suit.

Steel wool . . . A memory flickered for him. How you could set steel wool on fire even if it was damp. All you needed was . . .

A battery! And this whole suit ran on batteries, right?

He probed around some more, unlocking the chest symbol. All sorts of electronic goodies lurked in there, including a small battery nestled in the center of the circle. He pried it out and held it in his teeth as he slowly ripped out some of the steel wool.

Carefully, he wrapped the wool around a piece of concrete that had come down when he'd vibrated the rats away. It was long and slender, more a splinter than a chunk. He put the wool at the thicker end, held the slim end, and then—before he could lose his nerve—ran the battery terminals over the steel wool.

He expected an explosion of light, a big, catastrophic fireball. But instead he got a disappointing spattering of sparks that quickly died.

Wait. Disappointing? Heck, no! He'd just made light. Now he only needed to refine it.

Back into the costume. He had a source for fire; now he just needed something to keep it going. He finally found a seam and ripped away half the inside of his left sleeve. He wound that around the makeshift torch and touched the battery terminals to the steel wool again.

This time . . .

Oh, yeah!

The sparks leaped to the fabric, lay there for a moment, glistening, and then the fabric went up in flame. Wally shielded his dark-adjusted eyes until his pupils contracted. Slowly panning his torch around, he could make out the perimeter of the chamber and even perceive a shadow that just had to be a tunnel out.

"Ogg make fire," he grunted to himself. "Now Ogg get out of here."

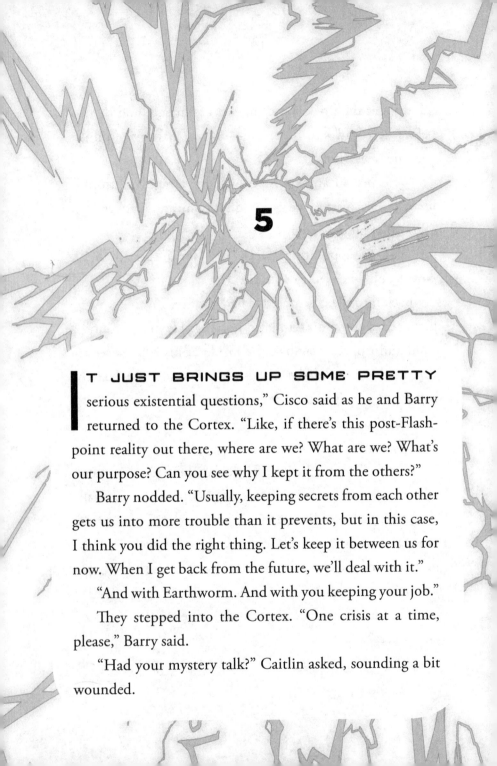

5

IT JUST BRINGS UP SOME PRETTY serious existential questions," Cisco said as he and Barry returned to the Cortex. "Like, if there's this post-Flash-point reality out there, where are we? What are we? What's our purpose? Can you see why I kept it from the others?"

Barry nodded. "Usually, keeping secrets from each other gets us into more trouble than it prevents, but in this case, I think you did the right thing. Let's keep it between us for now. When I get back from the future, we'll deal with it."

"And with Earthworm. And with you keeping your job."

They stepped into the Cortex. "One crisis at a time, please," Barry said.

"Had your mystery talk?" Caitlin asked, sounding a bit wounded.

"It was boringly technical," Barry told her. "When we start talking mitochondrial DNA and recombinant cytoplastic cell structures, you and I will step out and spare ourselves Cisco's glazed-over eyes."

That seemed to mollify Caitlin a bit, but H.R. still seemed miffed, arms folded over his chest, not a drop of coffee in sight. "What about me? What earns me a secret B.A. convo?"

"When I need the very best coffee the Multiverse has to offer," Barry said with great sincerity. "For now, though, I need to get to the future."

Cisco launched into lecturer mode again, turning to the dry-erase board. "OK, so there are a couple of ways to do this. I'm thinking we treat Hocus Pocus's wand like a source of reverse carbon-14 dating."

Radiocarbon dating—also known as carbon-14 dating—was a technique used by scientists to determine how old something was, Cisco explained. Most living things contained the isotope carbon-14 (also notated as ^{14}C). As time passed, the amount of ^{14}C diminished, decaying into nitrogen. The rate of decay for ^{14}C was constant, and since the ratio of ^{14}C in a thing and the amount of carbon-12 (^{12}C) that exists naturally in the atmosphere was normally the same, you knew that when it differed, it was because the living thing had died, changing its ^{14}C content.

"So when you measure the difference in ^{12}C and ^{14}C, you can come up with a date of when the living thing stopped living. Ta-da!" Cisco held out his hands, waiting for applause. Or maybe just acknowledgment that the others understood him. All he got was blank stares.

"What I'm proposing is almost the opposite," he continued. "Hocus Pocus's wand is from the far future: more than five millennia. Thanks to my vibe, we know exactly how many years will pass before the wand comes into being.

"This means," Cisco said, writing in great, looping characters on a new dry-erase board, "that we can calculate exactly where/when you need to travel. The wand has a specific set of vibrations, analogous to—"

"Wake me up when this is over," Caitlin complained.

"Not. Enough. Coffee. In the *world* . . ." H.R. slumped at a desk.

"Ignore them," Barry said. "I'm following you. The wand is like one end of a magnet. It'll draw me to the proper era."

"*And* to the proper alternate timeline out of the possible infinity of them," Cisco said with a significant arch of his eyebrows. "There are two problems, though. One I have a solution for."

"Hit me."

"Every object and living thing has a vibrational signature that aligns it with a time period and a universe. We travel to Earth 2, for example, by using the breaches or my vibe power to temporarily recalibrate our personal frequencies. But if you're going so far into the future, you're going to need to be disconnected from the present for a long time. I can handle that, I think. I give you a little vibe-boost with extra added Cisco Ramon flavor crystals, and your frequency should be all loosey-goosey and let you slip into any other time period for as long as you need."

Barry nodded. "Great. What's the other problem?"

Cisco wiped half the board clean and wrote in enormous letters: SPEED.

"Speed, my friend. This isn't one of your little side trips to yesterday. You're going to the long tomorrow, and for that, you need speed. You need lots of it. You need to sustain it. And you need more of it than you've ever had before if you want to run a few millennia into the future. And even H.R.'s most caffeinated of concoctions won't give you *that* kind of boost."

"I don't need it," Barry said confidently. "I learned a little trick on Earth 27, and it'll give me all the speed I need." He hesitated a moment. "You guys might want to shield your eyes. Sometimes things get lightning-y."

Cisco lowered his shades. Caitlin and H.R. each dutifully raised their hands, though with expressions of doubt.

Barry grinned and spoke the formula he'd learned on

Earth 27, the one that made Johnny Quick a speedster and made Barry Allen an even faster speedster. The key to Hyper-Heaven and greater speed!

"3X2(9YZ)4A!"

Nothing happened. He felt no faster. The world did not slow down.

"Waiting for the impressive stuff," Caitlin deadpanned.

"I was told there would be no math," H.R. complained.

Barry corkscrewed his lips into focused concentration. "Let me try again." He spoke the formula one more time, this time immersing himself in its nuances, in the way it described the multidimensional path to and from the Speed Force. "3X2(9YZ)4A!"

Still nothing.

"It's supposed to work!" he blurted out, suddenly terrified. How would he run so far into the future without the extra speed?

"I hear it happens to all speedsters sometimes," Cisco cracked, peering over the rims of his sunglasses. "Let's get real, shall we?"

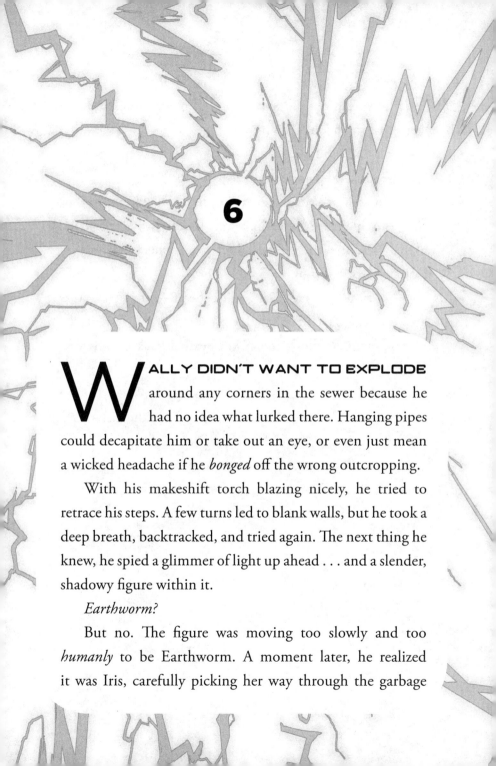

6

WALLY DIDN'T WANT TO EXPLODE around any corners in the sewer because he had no idea what lurked there. Hanging pipes could decapitate him or take out an eye, or even just mean a wicked headache if he *bonged* off the wrong outcropping.

With his makeshift torch blazing nicely, he tried to retrace his steps. A few turns led to blank walls, but he took a deep breath, backtracked, and tried again. The next thing he knew, he spied a glimmer of light up ahead . . . and a slender, shadowy figure within it.

Earthworm?

But no. The figure was moving too slowly and too *humanly* to be Earthworm. A moment later, he realized it was Iris, carefully picking her way through the garbage water toward him. She was so intent on watching her footsteps that she hadn't seen him yet.

"Iris!" he shouted.

She looked up and stumbled. "Wally?"

Before she could say anything more, he zipped to her side, caught her around the waist, then whisked her back along the tunnel and up the ladder, placing her safely next to a quite-surprised-looking Joe.

"No time to talk," Wally said. "See if you can seal this area off. There's a chamber down there where I saw Earthworm—get CSI down there. I'm headed back to S.T.A.R. Labs."

Joe didn't even get the chance to shout, "Hey! *I'm* the cop, not you!" before Wally had sped off into the distance.

Iris and Joe exchanged glances. "You ain't never allowed to get superpowers, baby," Joe told her very seriously. "I can't handle all *three* of you running around like crazy."

"That's sexist, Dad."

"Sexist? God, no. *Practical.* I'm just trying to stay alive." He dug into his pocket for his cell phone and started dialing CCPD numbers.

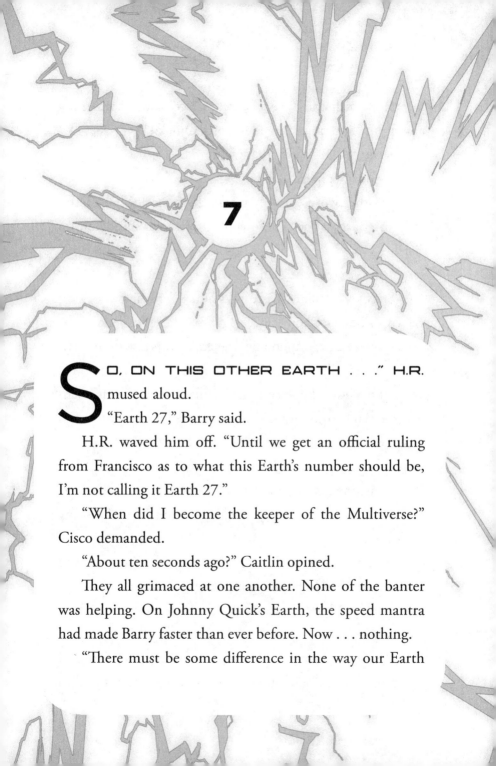

7

S O, ON THIS OTHER EARTH . . ." H.R.
mused aloud.

"Earth 27," Barry said.

H.R. waved him off. "Until we get an official ruling
from Francisco as to what this Earth's number should be,
I'm not calling it Earth 27."

"When did I become the keeper of the Multiverse?"
Cisco demanded.

"About ten seconds ago?" Caitlin opined.

They all grimaced at one another. None of the banter
was helping. On Johnny Quick's Earth, the speed mantra
had made Barry faster than ever before. Now . . . nothing.

"There must be some difference in the way our Earth

interfaces with the Speed Force," Cisco said. "Something about our local physics renders John Quickie's—"

"Johnny Quick," Barry interrupted.

"—formula inert."

"In other words, it only works there, not here," Caitlin said. "So Barry is back to Slowpoke Rodriguez speed here on Earth 1."

"Hey!" Barry protested.

"She's got a point," Cisco told him. "With just your own velocity, I don't see how you're going to be able to work up the necessary speed to go almost five thousand years into the future."

Barry gritted his teeth and bounced on his toes. He wanted to get to the sixty-fourth century *now*. Hocus Pocus was too dangerous and had been on the loose for too long. There was no time to waste. "I could draft off Wally's speed. If he were here."

"Someone say my name?" Kid Flash asked as he blew into the Cortex. "You guys bad-mouthing me behind my back again?"

With a huge grin, Barry held out his arms and hugged his younger brother, managing to ignore the sewer stench wafting from him. "I thought you were down in a hole somewhere."

"Came up for air." There was something too blasé and too calm about Wally's tone, but Barry allowed himself to ignore it for the moment. The sixty-fourth century beckoned. The defeat of Hocus Pocus. He could deal with whatever was bothering Wally when he got back.

"Now that Kid Flash is back," Cisco said, "this might work. Let me run some numbers and . . ." His voice faded as he disappeared down the corridor, still talking to himself.

"You're good?" Barry asked Wally.

"Yeah, yeah, everything's fine." He shook off Barry.

"Earthworm?"

Wally waved away the question. "You've got bigger fish to fry, right? Don't worry—I'm on the Earthworm thing. Getting close. Got some leads. What do you need from me? A boost? Is that what I heard on my way in?"

Barry's suspicion spiked. Wally was being a little *too* calm. He knew Kid Flash had gone into the sewers in pursuit of Earthworm, a killer who had left bodies all over Central City. And then S.T.A.R. Labs had lost contact with him. Joe and Iris were out in the field right then, looking for clues. And yet here was Wally.

"Iris to S.T.A.R. Labs." Barry's heart thrummed at the familiar voice coming over the Cortex comms system. "I'm on my way back. Any news from Barry?"

"I'm here!" Barry called. "I'm back!"

Iris's relief was palpable even over a cellular connection and a speakerphone. "Thank *God*. Is Wally with you?"

"Right here, sis," Wally said. "We're figuring out some stuff."

"Don't move too fast, you two. I'm on my way." She signed off.

". . . got it all figured out," Cisco said, rambling back into the Cortex as though he'd never left. He held a plastic container in one hand and gestured wildly with the other. "I use the wand to pick up the necessary vibrations from the sixty-fourth century and sort of 'preload' them into your bodily frequency. Then you run like mad, drafting off Wally, until you pop-goes-the-weasel into the future. Here's the important part: Once you're there, you have to maintain the vibrational frequency of the wand. Otherwise, you'll slip back through the time stream to the present, and we have to do the whole stupid thing all over again." He looked around the room. "Everyone got it?"

H.R. nodded gravely. "Perfectly!"

"Don't take this personally," Cisco grumped, "but no one cares if *you* get it."

"Is there a way *not* to take that personally?" H.R. asked, perplexed.

"I want to run some tests first," Caitlin said. "Make sure his time on Earth 27 didn't leave any lingering medical issues we should know about."

Wally and Barry and Cisco exchanged a look.

"C'mon," Wally said.

"Buzzkill!" Cisco taunted.

"I feel fine," Barry said. "I really do. And the sooner I get to the future, the sooner I'm done with Hocus Pocus and can help you guys with Earthworm."

"And maybe work on keeping your job?" Caitlin said with a little more snark than was necessary.

Oh. Right. His job. Barry had almost forgotten.

"The hearing is tomorrow," he said. "If everything works out as planned, I'll be back in the present mere seconds after leaving." It would be as if he was never gone at all. He would stop Pocus, come back to the twenty-first century, put his head together with Wally and Iris to stop Earthworm, then spend a relaxing night at home poring over CCPD rules manuals to figure out how to convince the disciplinary board to keep him employed the next day. Piece of cake.

"We handle the most dangerous case first," Barry said.

"Team Flash triage," H.R. agreed from the corner. He had located his drumsticks and now tapped them lightly together.

Barry shivered for just an instant, thinking of what Cisco had told him—that in an alternate timeline, H.R. had sacrificed his life to save Iris from the evil speed god Savitar, who'd turned out to be none other than Barry himself. It was enough to give him a headache on top of a headache.

"You just shivered," Caitlin crowed, leaping up. "'Feel fine,' my butt!" She approached him and jammed a thermometer into his mouth, then connected a medical gadget to a port under the Flash emblem on Barry's chest.

"Uh rurry fee fih!" Barry protested around the thermometer.

"Who uses oral thermometers these days?" Cisco wondered. "Use one of those infrared zappers that you just aim at the forehead—"

"Barry's unique physiology throws off infrared," Caitlin reminded him, "giving inaccurate readings. This is much better." She popped out the thermometer. "Perfectly normal."

"You sound disappointed," Barry told her.

"You'd think *something* would be wrong with you after jaunting across the Multiverse," she said, scrutinizing the readout from the costume. "What's the medical expert supposed to do if you can just bounce around reality and still have a perfect ninety-eight-point-six temperature and a BP of one-seventeen over seventy-one?"

"You can step back and let *physician* become *physicist*," said Cisco, brushing her aside. He handed Barry the plastic case he'd brought in with him. "Here. You'll need this on your trip to the future."

Barry looked down at the wand tucked into his belt along with the torn-off cowl. "Why? And what about fixing my costume?"

"No time!" Cisco bellowed. "Take this!" He shoved the case at Barry until Barry relented and accepted it.

"If I already have the wand, what do I need this for?"

Cisco opened his mouth to answer, then looked around, embarrassed. "Well," he said, lowering his voice. "I packed you a lunch."

Caitlin smirked and stifled a chuckle. Barry stared at the case, then pried it open. Peanut butter and jelly on whole wheat, from the looks of it.

"Lunch," he said. "Why? Do you think they don't have food in the sixty-fourth century?"

"Who knows?" Cisco threw his hands into the air in frustration. "I'm trying to think of every angle. Maybe they've evolved past the need for physical sustenance. Maybe they just swallow a pill. Whatever you do, if they offer you some Soylent Green, DO NOT EAT IT."

"Got it." He wrestled the cowl into place. It didn't quite fit perfectly, having been torn at the neckline by Johnny Quick, but it would do for now.

"C'mon," Wally said. "Let's get this show on the road."

Barry hesitated. Iris was on her way. She was on her way *right now*, and he yearned to see her, but . . .

But he would be right back. In less time than it took to go, he would be back.

He ambled over to the desk that Iris used when she was

in the Cortex. A playing card lay there. When he flipped it over, he immediately recognized it as the card he'd received from Madame Xanadu. The one piece of evidence he had that the woman existed at all, that she wasn't merely a figment of his imagination.

After a moment's thought, he tucked it into a safe pocket in the tunic of his costume. It wasn't much, but it was a connection to home right now. And it was pure mystery and maybe even magical. He didn't believe in magic, but he was willing to accept that it might help him.

"Let's make this happen," he said.

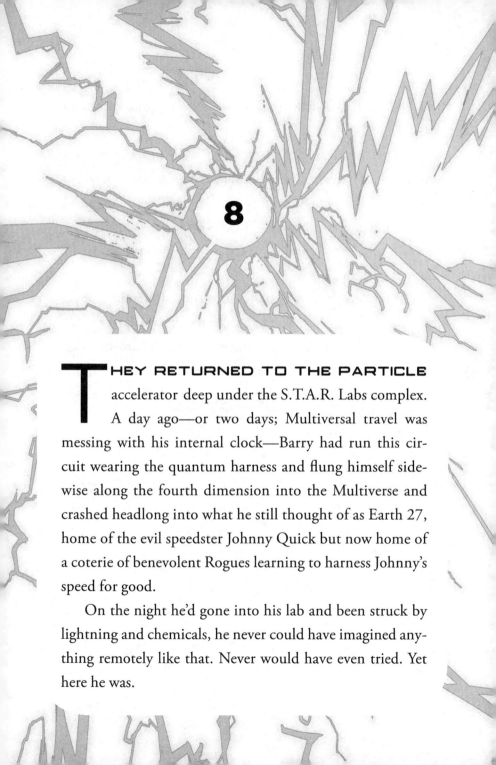

8

THEY RETURNED TO THE PARTICLE accelerator deep under the S.T.A.R. Labs complex. A day ago—or two days; Multiversal travel was messing with his internal clock—Barry had run this circuit wearing the quantum harness and flung himself sidewise along the fourth dimension into the Multiverse and crashed headlong into what he still thought of as Earth 27, home of the evil speedster Johnny Quick but now home of a coterie of benevolent Rogues learning to harness Johnny's speed for good.

On the night he'd gone into his lab and been struck by lightning and chemicals, he never could have imagined anything remotely like that. Never would have even tried. Yet here he was.

"OK," Cisco said, "so Wally starts off with a run, then Barry—"

"I get how it works," Barry said. "Wally picks up speed. I come in behind him and let his wake carry me, boosting me up to his speed without using my own. Then I cut around him—"

"I duck out of the way," Wally added.

"—and the combined speed of two Flashes sends me into the future."

If Cisco was hurt at being interrupted, he didn't let it show. Much. He checked the electronics on Barry's suit one final time, then secured the wand and the lunch with a new buckle he'd installed on Barry's left thigh. "Whatever you do, don't start running until I give you the vibe-push, got it?"

"Got it."

"Wally. Go."

The words weren't even out of Cisco's mouth, and Wally was gone.

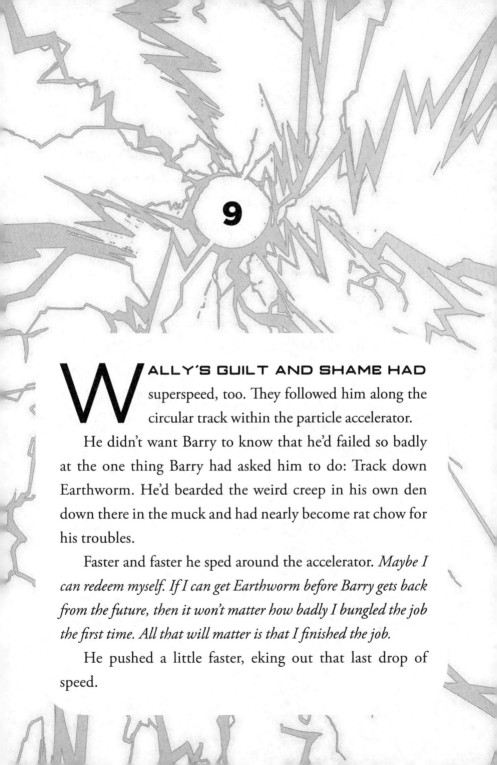

9

WALLY'S GUILT AND SHAME HAD superspeed, too. They followed him along the circular track within the particle accelerator.

He didn't want Barry to know that he'd failed so badly at the one thing Barry had asked him to do: Track down Earthworm. He'd bearded the weird creep in his own den down there in the muck and had nearly become rat chow for his troubles.

Faster and faster he sped around the accelerator. *Maybe I can redeem myself. If I can get Earthworm before Barry gets back from the future, then it won't matter how badly I bungled the job the first time. All that will matter is that I finished the job.*

He pushed a little faster, eking out that last drop of speed.

———

Cisco put one hand on Hocus Pocus's wand and the other on Barry's shoulder. Through some ineffable and unquantifiable process he couldn't explain (which drove him *crazy*), he could feel the different harmonics of the wand and of his friend. He closed his eyes, imagining two pebbles thrown into a still lake, one larger than the other. Two sets of concentric ripples moving at different speeds and with greater or lesser gaps between the wavelets.

In his mind, he forced those ripples to slow down, then to still, to freeze.

That was the easy part. The ripples represented Barry's frequency and the wand's. He'd "frozen" them both temporarily. Now to restart them, but with the same gaps and speed and ripples.

He gnashed his teeth and groaned. In his mind, the water started moving again, this time in perfect rhythm, the two splashes moving toward each other at the same time, about to overlap.

"Run," Cisco said, his voice hoarse. "Run, Barry, run."

Barry sped into the particle accelerator right behind Wally. It was the strangest feeling; he was going *so fast*, and yet he was hardly using any of his own energy. Wally's wake was pulling him along, and all he had to do was move his legs enough to keep from falling.

He felt untethered from reality. His personal vibrational harmony had been reset to match the wand's. He was in the twenty-first century, but his body yearned to be in the sixty-fourth. Something—the Speed Force, the time stream, the universe itself?—tugged at him, urging him on.

He let himself take another six hundred turns around the accelerator (it only took a couple of seconds), letting Wally's speed bear him along. Then, just as he and Wally came around a bend, Barry tapped Wally on the shoulder and peeled off to the right.

Kid Flash immediately juked to the left, getting out of Barry's way. Barry pumped his legs in earnest now, giving it his all. He channeled every last bit of speed in his body, adding it to the incredible momentum he'd already picked up thanks to Wally's run.

The world went invisible in an instant. Lights exploded all around him. A crack in the wall of reality split open before him, spilling out energy and power and colors no human eye had ever seen.

Without a picosecond of hesitation, Barry ran straight into it.

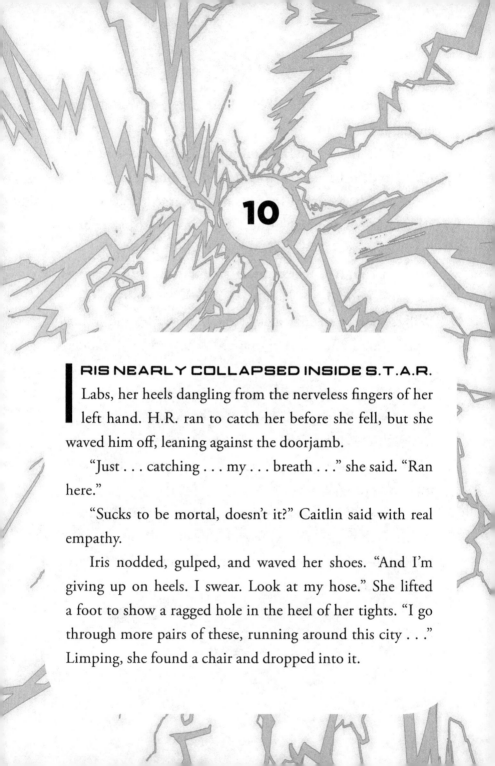

10

IRIS NEARLY COLLAPSED INSIDE S.T.A.R. Labs, her heels dangling from the nerveless fingers of her left hand. H.R. ran to catch her before she fell, but she waved him off, leaning against the doorjamb.

"Just . . . catching . . . my . . . breath . . ." she said. "Ran here."

"Sucks to be mortal, doesn't it?" Caitlin said with real empathy.

Iris nodded, gulped, and waved her shoes. "And I'm giving up on heels. I swear. Look at my hose." She lifted a foot to show a ragged hole in the heel of her tights. "I go through more pairs of these, running around this city . . ." Limping, she found a chair and dropped into it.

"Dad's securing what we think is Earthworm's latest crime scene. I came back here to see Barry."

"Just missed him!" Cisco announced cheerfully, striding into the Cortex with Wally at his side. "We just shotgunned him five millennia into the future." He frowned. "Or did we slingshot him?"

"I thought we boomeranged him," Wally said.

Iris struggled to her feet and stomped over to her brother and Cisco with as much outrage as her poor, battered soles could sustain.

"Are you crazy?" she demanded. "We almost lost him on Earth 27 already, and now you just let him run off to the future? Have you lost your minds?"

Cisco held his hands up defensively. "Hey, he's the Flash. It'll be fine. He'll be back in a second."

Iris planted her fists on her hips. "One," she intoned.

Cisco looked around and chuckled. "So, call it two seconds, then."

Still nothing. Iris's neck muscles vibrated in sheer rage. Cisco backed up. Wally took a few steps to the left, trying very hard to blend in with a wall.

"Give it a few seconds. There's, uh, always the possibility of relativistic noise perturbing the fourth-dimensional medium due to mismatched quark flavors."

"You just made that up."

"I might have. You can't prove it."

They waited.

Five minutes passed.

Nothing.

An hour passed.

Nothing.

11

NOW WHAT?" IRIS ASKED.

Cisco pursed his lips. "It's said that a good scientist is not afraid to say *I don't know*."

"And?"

"And I guess I'm a good scientist."

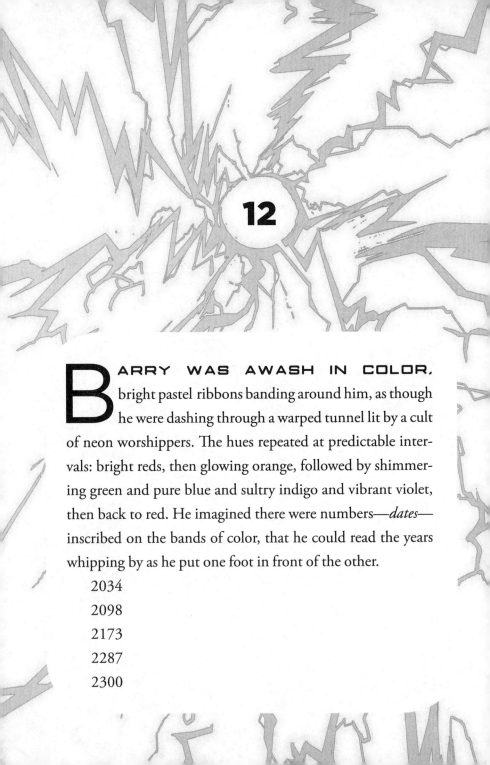

12

BARRY WAS AWASH IN COLOR, bright pastel ribbons banding around him, as though he were dashing through a warped tunnel lit by a cult of neon worshippers. The hues repeated at predictable intervals: bright reds, then glowing orange, followed by shimmering green and pure blue and sultry indigo and vibrant violet, then back to red. He imagined there were numbers—*dates*—inscribed on the bands of color, that he could read the years whipping by as he put one foot in front of the other.

2034
2098
2173
2287
2300

He didn't know what he was running on. What surface could there possibly be in the interstitial instants between instants themselves? The mere ideas of "surface" and of "running" had become metaphors; he was part of the quantum foam of the universe, using his personal vibrational harmonics to retune the universe around him into a new chord on the scale of reality.

The colors washed over him.

2319

2399

Years fell to his footsteps. Decades crunched underfoot.

2421

The twenty-fifth century. Birth time of Eobard Thawne. Barry was winded and not even half a millennium into the future. His lungs burned with whatever pretended to be air here in the time stream. Sweat ran down his forehead and cheeks, wicking away and sizzling in the impossible heat of time travel.

2501

2527

2540

He was definitely slowing down. Missing a step here and there. With a groan and a clench of his jaw, he pushed forward. Hocus Pocus had ordered him to kill an entire baseball stadium of innocent people! Only luck, quick thinking, and slow movement had saved the day and stayed his hand.

Slow movement . . . His hand drifted to the pocket where he held Madame Xanadu's card. No time for slowing down. No time for anything but running faster, farther, harder. He had to reach the sixty-fourth century. He had to learn the secrets of Hocus Pocus and make sure that that lunatic could never again threaten Central City.

2600

2610

2615

Barry cried out loud and forced himself forward, one foot in front of the other.

Just one foot in front of the other, Joe had said. A long time ago. Barry was starting to hear Joe's voice now, and he wondered—was he merely remembering this, or by running pell-mell through the time stream, was he somehow reliving it?

"You've got to beat the ball to first base!" Joe told Barry, who crouched in the dirt of the Little League field. Barry held up a hand to shield his eyes from the sun. Out there on the mound, the pitcher would soon go into his windup. Barry wasn't afraid of the pitcher. He had a good eye, and he could get the bat on the ball pretty well.

But he never made it to first base.

"You know how I always tell you to keep your eye on the ball?" Joe said. "Well, as soon as you feel that bat go shaky in your hands, as soon as you feel the impact, you forget all about keeping your eye on the ball. All that matters at that point is where *you* go. And how fast."

"I'm not fast enough," young Barry said, and in the time stream, the same words formed on his lips. Exhaustion was setting in. His legs felt as though someone had pumped liquid lead into their veins. The pain was excruciating and never-ending.

"You *are* fast enough," Joe told him. "You do it the same way everyone else does. One foot in front of the other. Forget the ball. Put your head down, and charge right up that baseline. One foot in front of the other. You get me?"

The thin crowd of parents and siblings was starting to get restless. Joe had called a time-out to buck up Barry at the plate. The umpire cleared his throat meaningfully.

Joe grinned and did that deep throat chuckle that Barry always associated with dumb jokes, old shows on TV, and ridiculous comments from Joe's CCPD partner. "You got this, son," he whispered, then straightened Barry's ball cap and stepped back.

"Game on!" the ump shouted.

"Game on," Barry whispered in the time stream.

2662

2670

Pumping legs. They were nerveless now, just wooden appendages dangling from his hips. He forced them to bend and flex through sheer willpower.

And somewhere/when in the past, somewhere/when in the eternal now, young Barry Allen swung the bat. The crowd's breath sucked in as one with the resounding *thwack* of the bat striking the ball. Not far enough for a home run or even a double. Not for Slowpoke Allen. But a single, surely. A base hit, right?

He threw the bat aside and ran, charging up the baseline, head down. The baseline blurred beneath him, and he imagined it had somehow become a rainbow of colors.

Barry focused on his feet. One foot in front of the other. One foot in front of the other. That's all it was. It was nothing complicated. It wasn't math or science or even lying awake at night, trying not to think of his father, locked away in Iron Heights for a crime he didn't commit.

He thought only of his feet.

2700

2743

2758

Forward.

Faster.

One foot in front of the other.

In the time stream, he was done, he knew. He'd gone as far as he could go, as fast as he could go. But back in the past, back in his personal history, he knew he had fewer than sixty feet from home plate to first base, and he was going to make it. This time, he wouldn't let Joe down, wouldn't let the team down, wouldn't let *himself* down.

"I'm gonna make it, Joe," he heaved into the soundless, airless void of the time stream. "If it kills me, I'm gonna make it."

The next thing he knew, he had collided—hard—with the first baseman, plowing through him, knocking the other kid over. He thought his numb legs felt something different, something not-dirt, send a shock up his bones, but then he heard the first-base ump shout, "Safe!" and he kept running, pumping his arms, his breath hot and raw, kept running, kept running into the outfield, one foot in front of the other, one foot in front of the other, until at last he could run no more and he collapsed in a dark, senseless heap.

Barry opened his eyes. Every part of his body hurt. Two blurry figures loomed over him. For an instant, he thought they were his team's first-base coach and Joe. Then one of them spoke:

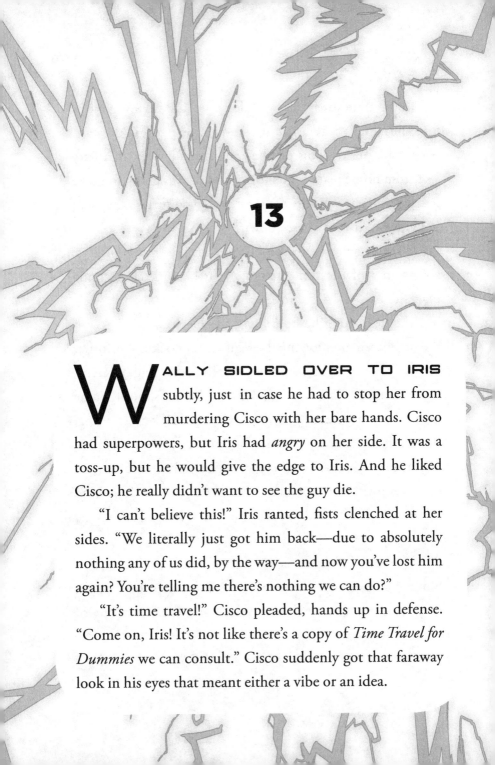

13

WALLY SIDLED OVER TO IRIS subtly, just in case he had to stop her from murdering Cisco with her bare hands. Cisco had superpowers, but Iris had *angry* on her side. It was a toss-up, but he would give the edge to Iris. And he liked Cisco; he really didn't want to see the guy die.

"I can't believe this!" Iris ranted, fists clenched at her sides. "We literally just got him back—due to absolutely nothing any of us did, by the way—and now you've lost him again? You're telling me there's nothing we can do?"

"It's time travel!" Cisco pleaded, hands up in defense. "Come on, Iris! It's not like there's a copy of *Time Travel for Dummies* we can consult." Cisco suddenly got that faraway look in his eyes that meant either a vibe or an idea.

"*Time Travel for Dummies*," he murmured. "I bet I'd make a mint."

Iris growled and flung out a hand. She picked up H.R.'s coffee mug from a nearby desk and hurled it at Cisco, who ducked, yelping. H.R. yelped, too, even more loudly. "My Moroccan blend!" he shrieked. "My Moroccan blend!" He rushed to where the mug had shattered against a wall, a dripping brown stain marring the pristine S.T.A.R. Labs paint job.

"Sweet, bitter baby," he moaned. "Daddy's gonna miss you. For the six to ten minutes it takes to brew a new cup."

Meanwhile, Iris had stalked to Cisco, backing him up against a wall. "I get it, Cisco. We do super-things here. We do mad science. But when did common sense and responsibility get thrown out the window?"

"Barry *wanted* to go . . ." Cisco said, shrinking back farther.

"And if Barry wanted to jump off the Novick Bridge, would you give him a shove?"

Wally put a hand on her shoulder. "Hey, Iris, calm—"

She spun around and slapped his hand away. "Don't you *dare* 'Hey, Iris' me, Wallace West! You helped shoot Barry into the future. I'm not exactly thrilled with you, either."

"It was all Cisco's fault, really," Wally said quickly, and stepped back.

"Thanks for the sellout, my man!" Cisco said.

"Where's Caitlin?" Iris asked, still fuming. "I need to talk to someone with a grain of sense in her head."

She glared around the room—Wally, stepping back again; Cisco, still against the wall; H.R. kneeling on the floor, distraught—and said, "And don't embarrass yourselves by saying any of you have any sense."

She turned on her heel and stalked out of the room, in search of Caitlin Snow.

"So, the boys are all idiots," Iris announced.

Caitlin looked up from the microscope on her lab bench, where she was studying a sample of Barry's blood. "I don't understand how Barry can bounce around the Multiverse and not show any sort of alien infection or antibodies in his blood. You'd think that there'd be *some* virus or bacterium on one of these Earths that would hop on for the ride. Unless the transit from Earth to Earth eliminates pathogens." She clucked her tongue absently. "I think we need to institute a quarantine protocol for cross-universal travel. These guys keep jaunting to other universes as if it's the corner bodega and . . . Wait a sec. Did you say the boys are idiots?"

Iris sighed. "Took you long enough to get there."

Caitlin smiled. "Sorry. I'm stuck in my own head today. What did they do now?"

"It's not what they did, really. It's their attitude. They're just not—"

"Not freaking out about Barry being in the future like you are."

"We don't even know if he's in the time stream or the future!" Iris threw her hands into the air in frustration. "It's not like anyone can go check, you know? And they're just so blasé about it, as though this sort of thing happens all the time and *I'm* the crazy one for being worried!"

Caitlin ran a hand through her hair and smiled grimly. "I can't say I'm any better. Here I am down in my lab, burying myself in work, all so that I can pretend my friend isn't lost somewhere in the future or the past or another universe or somewhere in between." She indicated the microscope. "It took me three seconds to determine that there's nothing wrong with Barry's blood, but I've been down here for an hour studying it, anyway."

For the first time since she'd been told that Barry had gone off gallivanting into the future, Iris felt the ball of stress that had frozen just above her gut thaw a bit. "What are we supposed to do? We can't just sit around and *wait*, can we? There has to be something."

"I don't know what," Caitlin told her resignedly. "All the reasons why we couldn't find him on Earth 27 go double for the time stream. I know it doesn't help to hear it, but in the end, we have to trust that Barry can figure out the where and when and how of getting back here."

Iris gnawed at her lower lip. "You're right. That doesn't help."

Caitlin pursed her lips, thinking. "Scones and coffee at C.C. Jitters? My treat?"

Iris shrugged. "You're getting closer."

A noise behind her made her turn around. There, in the corridor outside the lab, Cisco, Wally, and H.R. were all kneeling on the floor.

"So, uh, we're here on our knees . . ." Cisco began.

"Which isn't comfortable," H.R. put in.

"On our *knees*," Cisco continued with a scowl in H.R.'s direction, "to beg your forgiveness and offer our help."

"I don't know why I'm begging forgiveness," H.R. said. "I didn't do anything."

"Three kneeling dudes are better than two," Wally shot back in a voice that said, *Quiet!*

Iris leaned against the doorjamb. "The fire has burned low, boys. You can stand up."

"We sort of rehearsed this on our knees," Cisco told her.

"Then continue."

Cisco cleared his throat. "Sometimes you get thrown a curveball. Which I assume is a bad thing, knowing nothing about baseball. But there you have it. You never know where your path will take you. As in the case of Georg Wilhelm Richmann—"

Iris interrupted him with a long sigh. "The ball-of-lightning-to-the-forehead guy."

Cisco did a double take. "Does *everyone* know about this guy but me?"

"Barry talks about him all the time."

"Look, there's nothing we can do for Barry right now," Wally told her. "And all we can do is say you were right—we shouldn't have just shot him off into the time stream like that."

"We have total faith Barry is coming back to us even as we speak," Cisco said. "In the meantime, the only thing we can do is keep pushing through here in the present, doing the work *he* would do, if he were here."

A moment of silence passed, then another and another. Wally and Cisco both turned to glare at H.R. with mingled expectation and annoyance.

"Oh!" H.R. said. "My turn!" His brow furrowed. "I forgot my lines, guys."

Cisco buried his face in his hands. "I swear, I'm fleeing to Earth 2 and never coming back."

Wally stood up. "Before this gets any stupider . . . Look, Iris, we're gonna figure out this Earthworm thing, OK? I know it's not enough, and *nothing* is enough, but we love Barry, too, and we're hurting, too, and maybe this can take our minds off it. And even if it can't, it's what Barry would want us to do. Because he would be really pissed if he knew we were sitting around here yelling at each other when there are bad guys out there. He would want us to pull together and keep fighting the good fight."

Iris shook her head, and when she spoke, her voice was a hoarse whisper. "You're talking about him like he's dead."

Wally went to her, hesitated a moment, and then put his arms around her. "He's not. I know it. Don't ask me how, because I can't explain it. Maybe I feel it through the Speed Force. I don't know." He relinquished the clinch and held her at arm's length. "Please believe me."

Iris wiped tears from her eyes. "How can I not?"

Just then, Joe West came rushing down the hall, nearly out of breath. "*Here* you all are. I've been looking . . ." He glanced around. "Someone want to tell me why these jokers are kneeling?"

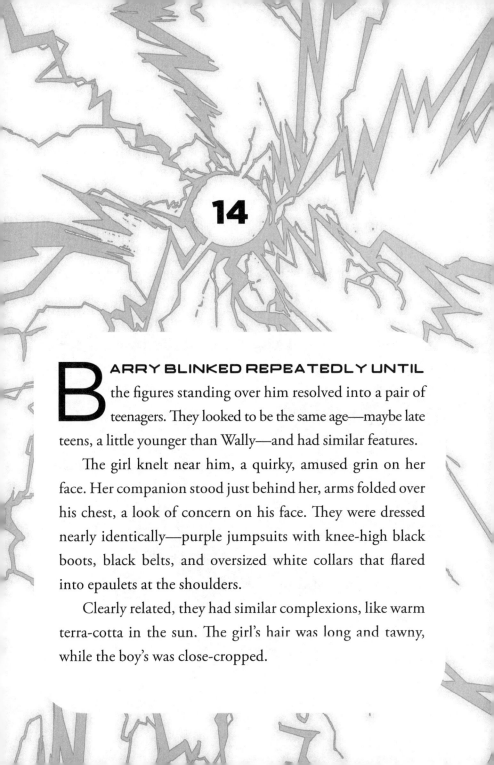

14

BARRY BLINKED REPEATEDLY UNTIL the figures standing over him resolved into a pair of teenagers. They looked to be the same age—maybe late teens, a little younger than Wally—and had similar features.

The girl knelt near him, a quirky, amused grin on her face. Her companion stood just behind her, arms folded over his chest, a look of concern on his face. They were dressed nearly identically—purple jumpsuits with knee-high black boots, black belts, and oversized white collars that flared into epaulets at the shoulders.

Clearly related, they had similar complexions, like warm terra-cotta in the sun. The girl's hair was long and tawny, while the boy's was close-cropped.

"⟨symbols⟩," the girl said, "⟨symbols⟩—"

"⟨symbols⟩," the boy growled. "⟨symbols⟩."

The girl rolled her eyes, as though used to him, and waved her hands dramatically. Barry realized that there was a haze of smoke and dust between him and them. As it cleared away, they could see him a little better, and vice versa. The girl's eyes widened, and the boy's cautious stance dissolved as his jaw dropped and he came a step closer.

"⟨symbols⟩," he said. "⟨symbols⟩."

The girl nodded but shrugged. "⟨symbols⟩."

Barry shook his head. Nothing was making any sense. What language were these two speaking?

"Do you speak English?" he asked. A thought occurred to him. "Like, twenty-first-century English?"

The two exchanged a glance that said, *Well,* that's *weird,* and then proceeded to babble to each other in their language some more.

Barry took advantage of the momentary lull to do a quick survey of himself. Although his entire body felt as though it had been pounded with rocks and then run along the world's largest and most aggressive washboard for a few hours, nothing seemed broken or permanently damaged. His legs prickled from toe to hip, coming alive with the worst case of pins and needles he'd ever experienced, so rather than stand, he settled for sitting up—slowly—and looking around.

Wow, he thought.

He was clearly in a city of some sort. Around him and off into the farthest distance he could perceive, buildings rose taller than any he'd ever seen before. They were made of no material he recognized; rather than being mortared together or assembled from sheets of glass or metal, they seemed to have been vacuum-formed somewhere and then air-dropped into place. Not a one of them had any sort of regular angle; they all were round or ovate at the base, and he realized with a shock that none of them seemed to have windows.

Their colors reflected a broad spectrum. He spied entire structures in chartreuse and lavender, bright metallic yellows, bold blues like a cloudless sky. It was a pop art festival of hues all around.

Between the buildings ran boulevards of some polished substance, pristine and burnished nearly white. Vehicles like hunched bugs drifted a foot or two over the streets. A few people peered out of the vehicles to take note of him, crumpled by the side of the road, but most ignored him.

Gazing farther up, he saw more streets, somehow floating in the sky, like ribbons strung among the buildings. Cars floated and glided up there, like fish suspended in an invisible aquarium the size of the sky.

Across the way, he spied a park, and the sight of trees—so simple and so familiar—filled him with relief.

Beyond the park, hovering hugely in the distance, the top of a massive sphere glowed and throbbed like a lesser sun.

"⏃⎐⌰⌿⏁⌿⎐⏚⎐⎅," the boy said, "⎐⎅ ⏁⌿⏅⏅⎅⎅ ⏚⏚ ⌿⏁ ⎐⏚⏚⏅⏁. ⏚⏁⌿⌿⏚⏚⎅ ⏁⌰⌿ ⏚⌰⎅⏚⌿⌿⏁⎅⌿ ⏚⏚⌰⏚⎅⌿ ⏚⌿⏁⌿ ⌰⌿⏚⏚⌿."

Barry sighed wearily. "English," he said again. Then, in desperation, "Français? Español?" His French and Spanish were rudimentary, but he would try anything.

The girl blew her hair out of her eyes and reached up to her left ear. A moment later, she held out her hand, palm up. A tiny bit of grayish plastic rested there.

"I don't get it," Barry said.

"⏚⌿⌿⎐ ⏚⎐⏁ ⏚⏁ ⏚⏚ ⌿⌿⎐⏚ ⏚⏚⏚," she told him and, at the same time, mimed putting the little doohickey back in her ear.

Barry swallowed and grinned. "Thanks, but if it's all the same to you, I'd just as soon not stick weird tech in my—"

With an exasperated sigh, she leaned over and pulled at his cowl. It came up too easily along his left ear, given the tear.

"No, no!" Barry said, but she slapped the thing at the side of his head, and he felt the little gadget slip nauseatingly into his ear canal.

Gross, he thought.

"Better?" she asked.

"Well, yeah," he said, "but not really *hygenic* . . . Hey! I can understand you!"

"No kidding," said the boy. "First-gen telepathic plug from DoxTech. The newer models are cooler, but this one will do for now. Now you can understand our Interlac."

Interlac. That was the name of their language. But wait, back up: *telepathic* . . . Was he actually *hearing* them speak, or was he reading their minds? Were they reading his?

He tugged the cowl back into place. Time to test his legs. Waving off help from the kids, he managed to stand up. It felt risky and also good.

The kids exchanged a look again. For the first time, the boy grinned.

"Someone is taking Barry Allen cosplay to an extreme, I see."

Barry frowned. "I *am* Barry Allen."

The girl giggled, and the boy shook his head. "No, no, not like *that*. It goes, *My name is Barry Allen, and I am the fastest man alive!* Now you try it."

Barry paused a moment, thinking it through. He peeled off the ragged cowl, which was beginning to fray at the edges. "But my name *is* Barry Allen," he said deliberately. "And I *am* the fastest man alive."

The boy shook his head again, clucking his tongue in disappointment. "Nope, still not right. You gotta *commit*—"

"Don!" the girl erupted. "Don, you idiot! *Look* at him!"

"I *am* looking at—"

"Bloody nass!" the girl said. "It's *him*."

Don swallowed hard halfway through a sigh, realizing. "Holy grife," he whispered. "It *is*. You're the Flash!"

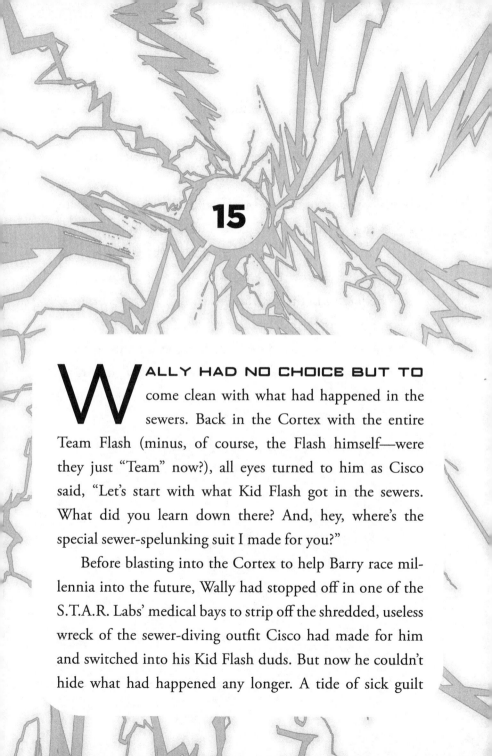

15

WALLY HAD NO CHOICE BUT TO come clean with what had happened in the sewers. Back in the Cortex with the entire Team Flash (minus, of course, the Flash himself—were they just "Team" now?), all eyes turned to him as Cisco said, "Let's start with what Kid Flash got in the sewers. What did you learn down there? And, hey, where's the special sewer-spelunking suit I made for you?"

Before blasting into the Cortex to help Barry race millennia into the future, Wally had stopped off in one of the S.T.A.R. Labs' medical bays to strip off the shredded, useless wreck of the sewer-diving outfit Cisco had made for him and switched into his Kid Flash duds. But now he couldn't hide what had happened any longer. A tide of sick guilt swelled within him, and he suddenly found himself studying his feet.

"Son?" Joe came up next to him. "Whatever it is, just tell us."

Wally drew in a deep breath and told them about his time in the sewer: how he'd gotten lost in the tunnels, then found Earthworm, only to succumb to the darkness and the twisting maze of the sewers. When he got to the part about being lost in the dark and the millions of rats heading toward him, Iris gasped and Joe stiffened.

"But I'm OK!" he protested, flinging out his arms as though to say, *See? I'm in one piece!* "Obviously! I got out!"

"And the suit?" Cisco asked. "Not to sound like I have a one-track mind or anything . . ."

Wally heaved a deep sigh and dashed away, returning an instant later with the remains of the suit.

"So, I had to, uh, do some cannibalizing in order to get out of the sewers . . ."

With a wounded cry, Cisco pounced on the ravaged outfit. "Baby! Baby! Come to Papa! Oh, the humanity!"

"Sorry," Wally mumbled as Cisco snatched the suit from him and raced off to a tech station.

"I saw him," Wally told them all earnestly. "He's real, and he's creepy as all get out. I even took a picture, but my phone's somewhere in the sewers under ten inches of the grossest, foulest water you can imagine." He hung his head. "I let you all down. I'm so sorry."

Joe put a hand on Wally's shoulder and squeezed reassuringly. "You did your best. And you can't beat yourself up for that."

"Thanks, Dad. I just wish my best had been better."

Iris gave him a hug. "At least now we know that Earthworm *was* in that area of the sewers. It's one more data point we can use to track him down."

"Hopefully before he kills someone else and steals their organs," H.R. said brightly.

Wally groaned. Not what he needed to hear. Anyone else who died now would be on his conscience.

Caitlin said, "Why don't we—"

"Yes!" Cisco cackled so loudly from the other side of the room that everyone jumped and Wally actually vibrated out of Iris's embrace. "You beautiful, beautiful hunk of technology! I would kiss you, if you didn't reek of sewer effluvia!"

"What's put the cream in your coffee, Francisco?" H.R. asked.

Cisco slapped his workbench in glee and laughed. Shoving off from the table, he coasted his wheeled chair to a rack of components, grabbed a cable, and drifted back to the suit.

"Wally, you said you took a picture of the guy, right?"

"Yeah, but it was with my phone. Which is gone. And

there's no way it backed up to the cloud from down there."

"Didn't need to!" Cisco chortled, plugging the cable into a concealed port in the costume. "You wrecked my darling but left her internals mostly intact. I had a local WiFi network running between your phone and the costume."

Wally blinked. He remembered what had happened right before he'd lost the phone: Earthworm pouncing on him from above, emerging from the darkness. Raising his phone . . .

"When I took a picture, it went to the suit?"

"I am the Redundant King of Redundancy," Cisco said. He shifted to a computer, and his fingers danced over the keyboard. "Give me a second . . ."

A moment later, the big screen lit up. Actually, *lit up* might have been the wrong way to put it: The image that Cisco pulled from the suit's backup system was dark, grainy, and murky.

Very plain in the center of it, though, was the face of Earthworm. Jaundice yellow, with its wrinkled forehead and bald yellow pate, it seemed to shine in the relative gloom of the sewer background.

"Nice shot," Joe marveled.

"The camera does all the work," Cisco said. "Autofocus, face identification . . ."

"Gee, thanks," Wally said wryly.

"I meant to say," Cisco said, "that, yeah, Wally got a nice

shot." Cracking his knuckles, he bent to the keyboard. He cropped the image around Earthworm's face. Some filters cleaned up the grain and made the face crisper. It was still hideous and grotesque, but now it was a very clean image of hideous and grotesque. "*Now* we have something to work with," Cisco said. "We figure out who this guy is, and we're one step closer to stopping Earthworm for good."

"Shoot a copy to my phone," Joe said. "I'll check it against CCPD records."

"Good idea," Iris said as Cisco fired off the copy. "Give me one, too, and I'll check the paper's morgue."

"Done and done," Cisco told them, still typing. "Meanwhile, I'll do a little hacky-hacky and run it through federal facial recognition databases, Interpol, and ARGUS. With any luck, between all of us, we'll have something in a few hours."

Caitlin cleared her throat. "Or you could save a lot of time and just ask me."

Cisco's fingers paused mid-typing. Joe and Iris, halfway to the door, paused and turned to her. H.R. raised his mug to his lips, grinning.

"Oh, this is gonna be *good*," he said.

Caitlin smirked as all eyes in the Cortex sought her out. "I know him," she said, shrugging as if to say, *No big deal.* "I can tell you his name."

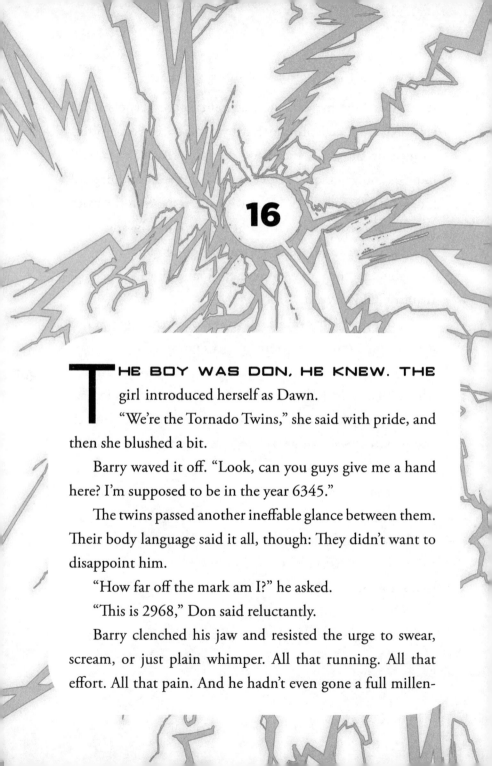

16

THE BOY WAS DON, HE KNEW. THE girl introduced herself as Dawn.

"We're the Tornado Twins," she said with pride, and then she blushed a bit.

Barry waved it off. "Look, can you guys give me a hand here? I'm supposed to be in the year 6345."

The twins passed another ineffable glance between them. Their body language said it all, though: They didn't want to disappoint him.

"How far off the mark am I?" he asked.

"This is 2968," Don said reluctantly.

Barry clenched his jaw and resisted the urge to swear, scream, or just plain whimper. All that running. All that effort. All that pain. And he hadn't even gone a full millennium into the future. Aiming for the sixty-fourth century, he'd ended up in the late thirtieth.

"Look," Dawn said, "we shouldn't really stand around here. The Science Police will show up soon."

"Science Police?" Barry was intrigued. Talk about combining the things he loved!

"Yeah, the Science Police," Don said. "They investigate, you know, science."

"Anomalies," Dawn amplified. "And you popping out of the time stream, spraying chronometric energies everywhere in the middle of the Kanigher Cross-Ave, is gonna spike some readouts at the Time Institute and SP HQ for sure."

"Kanigher . . ." The name was all too familiar to him, plastered on schools and roads in his own time. "So I'm still in Central City?"

Don shrugged. "Kinda. It's technically a supersuburb of the Megalop—"

"Time for geography later," Dawn interrupted. "Let's beat feet. Think you can keep up?" she asked Barry.

He chuckled ruefully. Apparently tales of his speed had not survived the intervening centuries intact. The "Tornado Twins" would learn soon enough. "You lead on. I'm sure I can follow."

And then—much to his shock—both kids took off at astounding superspeed.

It took him a moment to overcome his surprise. And then another to berate himself for being a complete idiot. They called themselves the *Tornado* Twins. Of *course* they had speed. *Barry, you're an idiot!*

By that point, almost a full second had passed. The Tornado Twins were two purplish blurs on the horizon. Barry ran after them, cursing every step as his still-sore legs pumped. Nonetheless, he wasn't about to let a couple of teenagers outrun him. He pushed through the pain and poured on the speed, catching up to them in no time at all.

"Not bad!" Don said admiringly.

"Do I live up to the legends?" Barry asked.

"So far!" Dawn said. "This way!"

She zigged left sharply and vibrated through a glimmering violet wall. Even though all his instincts cried out not to—*Do NOT vibrate through walls when you don't know what's on the other side!* he'd told Wally more than once—he followed along with Don. An instant later, the three of them were in a cozy space with walls and a ceiling that curved around like an igloo's. Only the floor was flat and true.

Light glowed along a series of pinpoints that patterned the ceiling and upper portion of the walls, such that the room had no harsh shadows or dim spots. The furniture *floated.* Tables and things that looked like beanbag chairs but were made of clouds drifted along. Dawn flung herself onto one of them, and it locked into place.

Barry stood in the middle of it all and took it in. In addition to the tables and weird chairs, there were also what appeared to be display cases. They clung to the walls and occasionally swapped positions with one another, whether guided by some kind of artificial intelligence or a preprogrammed system, he couldn't tell.

Artificial intelligence . . .

"Gideon?" he whispered.

Don laughed. "Wow, *that's* a blast from the past. You think there's a Gideon somewhere in the system, Dawn?"

Dawn shrugged. "Dunno. They purged a lot of the pre-revolution AIs after the—" She broke off.

"After what?" Don asked. He was rummaging in what appeared to be a cooler of some sort. "After the Great—"

Dawn zipped over to Don, slapped him upside his head, then zapped right back to her seat.

"Ow!" Don complained.

"You'll have to forgive my brother," Dawn said sweetly. "He was born thirty-one seconds later, and he's still trying to catch up. There are things we shouldn't tell you. Preserving the time continuum and all that."

That made abundant sense. He didn't want to know too much about his own future. The time stream seemed fragile enough as it was, and Cisco's admonition about alternate timelines and such seemed suddenly more important. He didn't want to fracture the timeline and make returning home even more difficult.

"Let's watch the finals!" Dawn said to no one in particular, and suddenly a hologram burst into view in the center of the chamber. It was in full color, partly translucent, with resolution and color fidelity that made reality look fake. No matter where Barry stood in the room, the hologram always seemed to be "facing" him.

A youngish man with a sweep of black hair grinned at him, holding up a sleek bottle of some sort.

"—Rokk Krinn here," he was saying brightly, "and when I get sweaty on the magnoball court, I recharge with a cool, frosty bottle of Polar—"

"Mute until the match is back on!" Dawn called, and the volume muted. "Stupid commercial."

Well, some things never changed, it appeared.

Barry glanced around some more. There were floating "newspapers" like those he'd seen in Thawne's time vault hidden in S.T.A.R. Labs. Some of them had English headlines, and he could read them. A few were familiar: FLASH HALTS GORILLA WAR! and RAINBOW RAIDER: LIGHTS OUT!

Others made no sense to him: THINKER STRIKES AGAIN! and ELONGATED MAN SOLVES LOCKED ROOM MYSTERY and KID FLASH JOINS TEEN TITANS.

He started thinking again about alternate timelines, about Cisco's concerns. What if he wasn't just in the thirtieth century . . . but the *wrong* thirtieth century? What if this was some sort of offshoot?

He had to trust that Cisco's vibe pattern would keep him going in the right direction and that the wand would act as a compass for him.

All water runs to the sea, he reminded himself. Eventually, there had to be a place where the timelines met.

"So, is this where you kids live?" he asked.

"Nah." Don handed Barry a slim flask of liquid.

Barry considered demurring, but when he looked down for the lunch Cisco had packed for him, he discovered that the plastic container had been crushed beyond recognition during his run to the future. And he *was* hungry. And thirsty.

It took a moment for Barry to figure out how to open the flask—you bent the top in one direction, then another, and a little straw popped out—and the blue substance inside was sickly sweet when he drank it. "Special electrolyte compound," Don told him. "For speedsters."

Barry guzzled gratefully.

"This is more like a hangout," Dawn said. "When . . . you know, when our parents annoy us, we come here."

"How did you get your speed?"

"Eh, the usual," Dawn said airily. "A little chemistry, a little electricity. A certain genetic predisposition. Nothing exciting."

"Zap, boom!" Don said. "Don and Dawn, the Tornado Twins!"

"Do people have last names in the future?"

Don threw his hands up into the air. "Holy grife! Do you want our help or our biographies?"

Barry wondered if maybe he'd stumbled into some kind of thirtieth-century taboo. "Sorry. Just making conversation while I recharge." He took another slug of the grossly sweet fluid and felt it spread through his body, reinvigorating cells, repairing damage.

Something caught his attention out of the corner of his eye.

"Hey, I've seen something like this before!" He tapped on a clear dome resting over a fabric-covered stand. On the stand was a golden ring emblazoned with a Flash lightning insignia. "Actually, I *have* one." He stripped off his right glove and held up his hand. There, on the ring finger, was a ring just like the one in the case. He'd taken his from Eobard Thawne, the Reverse-Flash, after defeating him, and had been wearing it regularly since. Thawne had somehow stored his costume inside the ring. Barry had asked Cisco to do the same with his costume, but Cisco hadn't figured it out yet.

"Wait a sec," he said, leaning in to scrutinize the ring in the case. "Or is *this* the same one I'm wearing, just centuries later? Is that even possible for it to exist twice in the same time period?"

"Ow!" Don exclaimed. "Ontological paradox makes my head hurt." He gripped his temples in an overwrought attempt at comedy. "Next you'll be asking if it's OK to kill your own grandfather and ride the paradox wave into a new timeline."

"Wasn't planning on asking any of that." But he couldn't help thinking of the *other* Barry Allen, the Flashpoint Flash. That Barry had mucked with history and paid a dear price. Barry had no intention of doing the same.

"Look, kids, I appreciate the drink and the future history lesson, but at this point, I have to be realistic about my options."

Don settled into one of the cloud chairs and drifted nearby. Barry couldn't fathom lounging on a cloud, and so he remained standing. In short, clipped sentences, he explained about Hocus Pocus, his reign of terror over twenty-first-century Central City, his capture, and his eventual escape from the inescapable Pipeline.

The twins nodded along at certain points. Some of this was familiar to them. He glanced around their hangout again, at the floating newspapers. Flash fans? Historians? It didn't matter; they knew him and his past and his speed. If anyone could help, they could.

Cisco's vibe had stabilized him for the time trip, but at this point . . .

"At this point," he admitted, "my only option may be to cancel out the vibe, return to the twenty-first century, and try again some other way. Maybe Cisco can whip up something—"

Don shook his head violently, and Dawn waved her hands frantically, saying, "No, no, no, no!"

"Don't go back," Don said. "I think we can help you figure out how to get farther into the future without blowing out your legs again. There's been a lot of research in time travel in the past few years. Guys like Dox and Vidar and Senius have really upped the game."

"Building off research begun in your own period," Dawn hastened to add. "You and Cisco Ramon really kick-started what's thought of as the ante-modern time travel movement."

Barry accepted the compliment but shrugged. "I don't need you to stroke my ego. I just need a way to get to the sixty-fourth century and figure out what's what with Hocus Pocus."

Don and Dawn did their twin-thing again, that shared, indefinable glance that seemed to communicate so much more than the time elapsed would indicate. Speedsters were fast; twins were faster. At transmitting ideas, at least.

"We think our first move is the university," Dawn said after the shared moment. "We can help with a couple of things there. Fix up your costume, for one thing."

"Kids, that's nice of you, but I need a physicist, not a tailor."

"Hey!" Don hopped down from his cloud-chair and planted his fists on his hips. "You're *going* to get to the sixty-fourth century, and when you arrive, do you want to look like the living legend you are, or do you want to look like you left your nice costume back in the prehistoric twentieth century?"

Barry couldn't help chuckling at the kid's verve and passion. "You might have a point. But I don't think you can really call it prehistoric"—he gestured to the newspapers—"and it's the twenty-*first*, not the twentieth."

Don blushed. "Right. My bad. Sorry."

"Let's just call it a mopee," Dawn suggested.

"What's a mopee?" Barry asked. The plug in his ear had given him the word but not its meaning.

"That," Don explained, "is when something happens and everyone knows it, but we all pretend it didn't."

"Fine by me. It's a mopee. Never happened."

Don relaxed. He chugged the last of his drink and said to Dawn, "Professor Giffitz?"

She nodded. "Let's go."

They ran so fast through the streets of future Central City that Barry hardly had time to study it. The roads were seamless and felt slightly plastic, with a pleasing give that made running on them easier. Were there so many speedsters in the future that they'd designed special roads for them? Nah, he couldn't believe that. But he enjoyed the coincidence.

The buildings blurred by, a polychromatic kaleidoscope of towers and turrets.

"How do you guys know a university professor?" Barry asked at one point.

"He's our instructor in Superthermoplastic Design this semester," Don explained.

Barry blinked. "You kids are in *college?*"

"Why not? We're sixteen."

Oh. The future. Where teenagers studied superthermoplastic design in college. Of course. Barry said nothing more.

"We just skim around that," Dawn said, pointing, "and the university's on the other side."

She gestured to the massive bulk of the hemisphere he'd noticed earlier. This close, it was even bigger, a gigantic, impossibly smooth dome surrounded by an enormous park. Even at their speed, it would take a few seconds to detour around.

"Why not run over it?" Barry asked. "Or through it?"

Don nearly choked. "That's the fusion powersphere!"

"It provides clean energy to the entire region," Dawn explained. "If you ran *through* it, well . . . a few of your atoms might make it out on the other side, but I kinda doubt it."

"And it's illegal to run over it," Don said. "They, uh, they kinda passed that law just for us, but it probably applies to you, too."

If Barry had gotten his powers at sixteen instead of in his twenties, he could imagine all sorts of trouble he might have gotten into. It made perfect sense that this era had to clamp down a little on the Tornado Twins. *Good kids*, he thought, *but still kids.*

They skirted the perimeter of the "fusion powersphere." It sounded horribly dangerous, and yet the future had decided to plop it right in the middle of the city, with some absolutely stellar landscaping around it. Fusion power was generally safer than fission, he knew—less chance of radiation leaks, for one thing. In his own time, no one had yet made fusion power practical, but here in the thirtieth century, it seemed as though the energy scientists knew what they were doing.

Still, safe as it must have been, he kept a distance as they circumnavigated the bulk of the powersphere.

On the other side, the city opened up into a breathtaking space that nearly stopped Barry in his tracks. He was almost a thousand years in the future, yeah, but he recognized a college campus when he saw one. Even one where the buildings were . . .

. . . floating!

The campus itself was a wooded field that stretched for several acres in all directions. Pathways cut among the trees and across great swaths of green grass. Students milled about in the shadows of the trees and of the buildings that levitated thirty feet above the ground.

He followed Don and Dawn as they raced down a gentle slope. Finally, though, he called to them to stop for a moment so that he could stand and stare. The buildings varied in color from burnished gold to bright silver, each a rhombic prism with the rounded corners he'd already come to associate with this era's specific architectural language. He knew he probably looked like a rube, a hick, one of those tourists to the big city who couldn't stop staring up at the skyscrapers, and yet . . .

The buildings were *floating!* How could he *not* stop and stare?

Someone—some *genius*—had plotted out the hovering structures' positions so that they didn't block all the sunlight. The park beneath the buildings seemed no darker than any random city block Barry had ever strolled. Maybe they used some sort of reflective alloy on the outside of the buildings to enhance and direct the sunlight, too. Maybe . . .

The scientist and the aesthete in him were both in awe. The university blended science, art, and the environment in such a seamless fashion that it would be impossible to imagine any of those elements separate from the others.

The beauty of it brought a tear to his eye.

"Is everything OK?" Dawn asked.

"It's just . . . amazing." Barry immediately felt like a loser for using such a small word for something so powerful. Iris would have had a better word, he knew, and the thought of her jabbed at his heart. He hadn't seen her since leaving for Earth 2, and while it had only been a day or two, the jump into the Multiverse, his adventures on Earth 27, and now his trip to the future made it feel as though it had been years since he'd seen her, touched her face, held her in his arms.

He wanted to go home. He wanted to rest.

But he was the Flash.

"It's just the university," Don said. "No big."

How easy it was to get used to miracles, Barry thought. He'd become accustomed to his speed in short order, and here in the future, a sight that would trigger a million Instagrams in his own time wasn't even worth commenting on.

"Let's go meet this professor of yours," he said. Because as much as he admired the future, he wanted to end this nonsense with Hocus Pocus and get back to where he belonged.

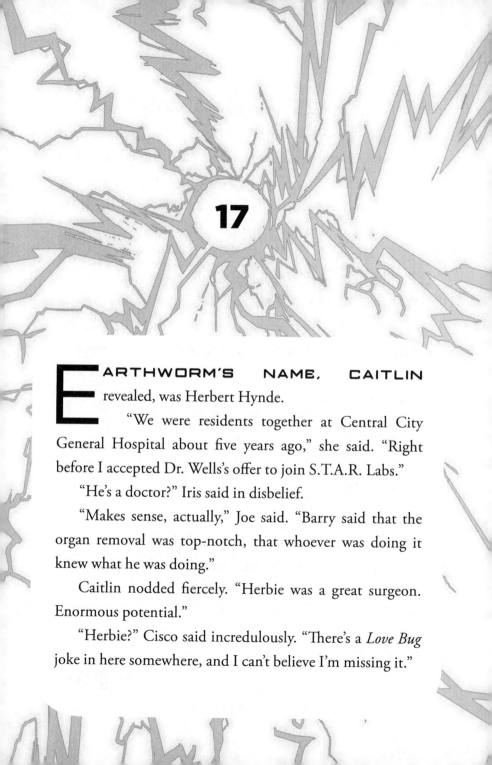

17

EARTHWORM'S NAME, CAITLIN revealed, was Herbert Hynde.

"We were residents together at Central City General Hospital about five years ago," she said. "Right before I accepted Dr. Wells's offer to join S.T.A.R. Labs."

"He's a doctor?" Iris said in disbelief.

"Makes sense, actually," Joe said. "Barry said that the organ removal was top-notch, that whoever was doing it knew what he was doing."

Caitlin nodded fiercely. "Herbie was a great surgeon. Enormous potential."

"Herbie?" Cisco said incredulously. "There's a *Love Bug* joke in here somewhere, and I can't believe I'm missing it."

"I can't believe Caitlin is on a cute-nickname basis with a sewer-dwelling serial killer," H.R. said very matter-of-factly.

With a toss of her head, Caitlin sniffed at him. "I haven't seen him in years. Last I knew, he was still at CCGH. When I moved over to S.T.A.R. Labs, a lot of things changed for me. I lost track of my old friends."

No one spoke for a moment. They knew that "a lot of things changed" included Caitlin becoming engaged to Ronnie Raymond, who had worked as an engineer at S.T.A.R. Labs. Ronnie had been thought killed in the particle accelerator explosion that had set off a wave of metahumans, but he'd actually ended up merged with a man named Martin Stein to become the hero called Firestorm.

Sadly, Ronnie perished saving Central City from the singularity formed by Team Flash's first major victory, the defeat of Reverse-Flash. Ronnie died a hero again, and his death weighed on everyone at S.T.A.R. Labs every day, none more so than Caitlin.

"He was a truly brilliant surgeon," Caitlin said, breaking the silence. "I can't imagine what would have driven him to . . . this." She gestured to the screen, where Earthworm glared out at them.

"He was . . . pretty far gone," Wally said as gently as possible. "Dude sicced a million rats on me, you know?"

"I think you have to prepare yourself for the likelihood that your friend Herbie is gone forever," Iris said. "Earthworm's all that's left."

Caitlin nodded. "I know."

Cisco strummed his fingers on his desk for a moment. "Spell his name?" he asked.

Caitlin did so, and Cisco punched it into the computer. A moment later, a photograph of Dr. Herbert Hynde came up on the screen. He was in his late twenties, with a receding hairline, flyaway brown hair, and bags under his eyes. He was the same guy Wally had seen, just not yellow and not as haggard looking.

"This is his ID photo for CCGH," Cisco said.

"Did someone not tell him it was picture day at school?" Wally joked.

"We worked twenty-hour shifts," Caitlin told him. "There wasn't a lot of time to pretty up."

"Sorry," Wally mumbled.

"According to the personnel database at CCGH," Cisco said, scanning the screen before him, "Dr. Hynde was put on suspension about four years ago, then terminated shortly thereafter."

"Is there a cause listed?" Iris asked.

Cisco shrugged. "A whole lot of legalese and medicalese." He cocked his head in Caitlin's direction. "Dr. Snow? Wanna take a crack at it?"

He surrendered his chair to Caitlin, who sat down and scrutinized the text Cisco had pulled from Hynde's employment file.

"Well," she said after a few moments, "reading between the lines, it looks like he stopped showing up for work. So they suspended him. Hospitals don't like firing doctors, if they can avoid it. It makes it look like maybe something untoward was going on and maybe gives people ammunition in lawsuits. But when he didn't show up after six months, they fired him and revoked his security pass."

"Wait." Joe came over to the computer and looked over her shoulder. "He never went back to the hospital? They fired him sight unseen?"

"Yeah. Seems like."

Joe skimmed the text, too. "Oh, man. Look." He pointed to the screen.

Caitlin followed his finger and smacked her forehead. "I can't believe I missed that."

"Missed what?" Cisco asked, looking as well. "Oh. Oh!"

The last time anyone at the hospital had seen Herbert Hynde was three days after the explosion of the particle accelerator.

"He *is* a meta!" Cisco breathed.

"Makes sense," Wally said. "I mean, I'm pretty sure he

was actually *talking* to those rats. And not like we might talk to one. I think they listened to him."

Iris started ticking things off on her fingers. "So, one: Hynde gets hit by the dark-matter wave and develops superpowers."

"Creepy, icky superpowers," H.R. amended.

"Two," Iris went on, "he spends a few days trying to live his old life, but . . . something happens. Which leads to three: He stops going to work and heads for the sewers."

"That's the part that doesn't make any sense," Caitlin said. "Herbie was a great doctor and an *empathetic* one. Not all doctors are so compassionate. If he got superpowers, why would that cause him to go underground?"

"Literally!" H.R. put in.

"Something happened in those few days," Joe mused aloud. "Something changed him from Dr. Kildare to Dr. Frankenstein."

"Dr. Kildare?" Cisco asked, baffled.

"Who?" said Iris and Wally at the same time.

"Is he an MD or PhD?" Caitlin wanted to know.

"Is he a villain, like Dr. Kill-Dare?" H.R. asked.

Joe threw his hands up into the air. "Fine! I'm old! Is that what you all wanted to hear?"

Iris and Wally grinned at each other. "It helps."

"Smart-aleck kids," Joe grumbled. "Look, he went from good guy to bad guy. There's got to be a reason. Caitlin, you had gone to S.T.A.R. Labs by then, but he had to have had other friends, right? Someone must have noticed something."

She closed her eyes tightly. "Nathan Markson. Denise Bernstein. That's all I've got, guys. Like I said before, residency is brutal."

"We'll start there," Joe said. "Iris, you and Cisco take one. Caitlin and I will take the other."

"Hey! What about me?" Wally demanded.

"And me!" H.R. demanded, a little less angrily.

"Wally, we need to hold you in reserve, in case Earthworm strikes again. Wait here for a signal. And, H.R., someone has to be here when Barry gets back." Joe looked around the room, settling at last on Iris. "Because he *is* coming back."

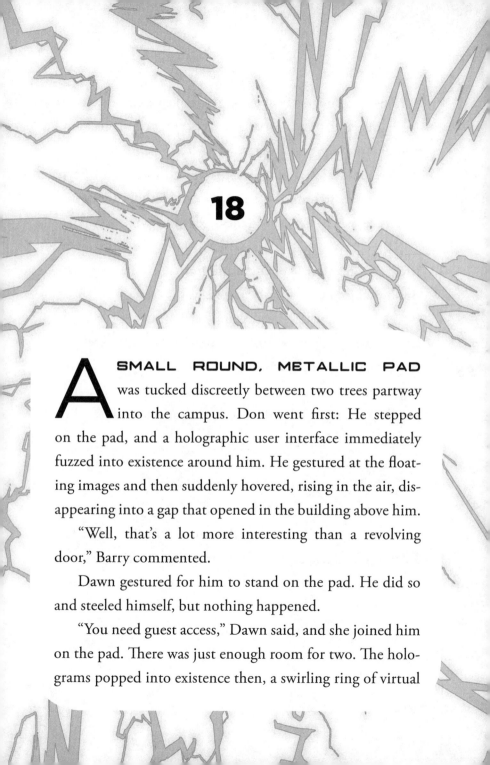

18

ASMALL ROUND, METALLIC PAD was tucked discreetly between two trees partway into the campus. Don went first: He stepped on the pad, and a holographic user interface immediately fuzzed into existence around him. He gestured at the floating images and then suddenly hovered, rising in the air, disappearing into a gap that opened in the building above him.

"Well, that's a lot more interesting than a revolving door," Barry commented.

Dawn gestured for him to stand on the pad. He did so and steeled himself, but nothing happened.

"You need guest access," Dawn said, and she joined him on the pad. There was just enough room for two. The holograms popped into existence then, a swirling ring of virtual buttons and sliders. Dawn's fingers poked and prodded at the lights, and then Barry's stomach dropped as he found himself floating gently up into the air.

The underside of the building irised open, and Barry and Dawn drifted inside. The floor closed under them, and gravity returned, depositing them gently on their feet.

Barry had a million questions. About the holographic computer interface. About the antigravity. About *everything*. But he kept them to himself. There was no time.

Don was nowhere to be seen. They found him a moment later in what appeared to be a combination office/laboratory, where he waited with an older man with gray hair and a gray handlebar mustache. The older man wore a light purple tunic with a flared collar and a square of white fabric stitched over his chest.

The technology was amazing, but Barry had to admit that thirtieth-century fashion left something to be desired.

There was someone else in the room, he realized—a young man perhaps as old as the twins. A bit portly, he had an unruly thatch of black hair and wore a skintight blue one-piece with white accent bars at the collar, waist, and arms.

"Professor Giffitz," Don said, "may I introduce—"

"Our visitor from the past," the older man said. "It's a pleasure."

They shook hands. "The twins said you might be able to help me with my costume."

"Of course, of course," Giffitz said, nodding vigorously. "I was just in the middle of something. One moment, please."

He looked over a table and selected a flask, then gestured to the boy in blue. "My assistant," he told Barry. "Charles Taine."

So they *did* have last names in the thirtieth century.

"Call me Chuck," the boy said amiably.

Giffitz handed the flask to Chuck. "Deliver this new discovery of mine, an instant, super-plastic fluid, to the Science Council, at once!"

"Yes, sir!" Chuck said. "Right away!!"

Once Chuck left, Giffitz leaned back on the table and stroked his jaw. "So, there's obvious damage to the cowl. I can fix that easily enough."

"Great." It was a minor thing, but it would be good to race into action with his costume intact. "I appreciate that a lot. Not to be ungrateful or anything, but what I really need is to get to the sixty-fourth century."

Giffitz blinked rapidly several times. "Young man, I specialize in hyperelastic materials science, not chronophysics."

"We'll be dealing with the time travel stuff," Don said hurriedly to Barry.

"Don't worry—we have something in mind," Dawn added. "We just thought you might want to have your costume fixed first. And, well . . ." She drifted off and looked away, almost embarrassed.

Barry did his best to tamp down his annoyance. The twins were trying to help, in their own way. But their priorities were way out of line.

"And what?" he asked.

"Show him the ring," Don said.

The ring? Oh, right. Barry slipped off his right glove and held up his hand so that Giffitz could see the lightning insignia ring he wore. "I don't see what this has to do with anything, though."

Giffitz nodded thoughtfully, studying the ring. "I think I see what you want. Give me a few moments." He cleared his throat. "And your costume. I'll need that, too."

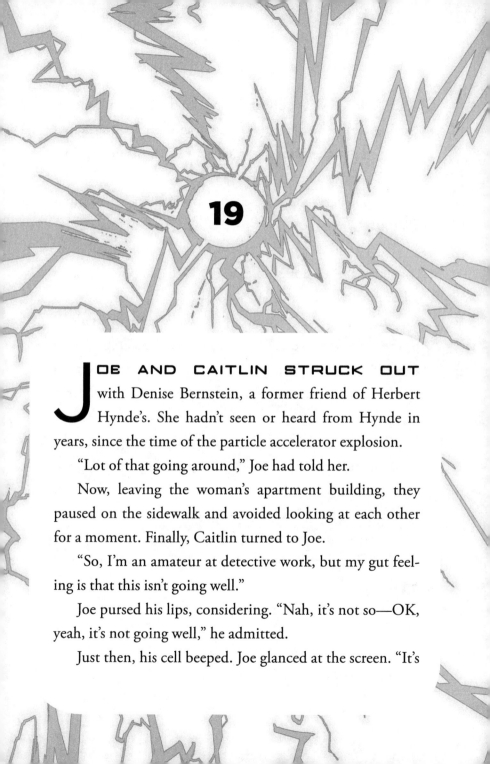

19

JOE AND CAITLIN STRUCK OUT
with Denise Bernstein, a former friend of Herbert
Hynde's. She hadn't seen or heard from Hynde in
years, since the time of the particle accelerator explosion.

"Lot of that going around," Joe had told her.

Now, leaving the woman's apartment building, they
paused on the sidewalk and avoided looking at each other
for a moment. Finally, Caitlin turned to Joe.

"So, I'm an amateur at detective work, but my gut feeling is that this isn't going well."

Joe pursed his lips, considering. "Nah, it's not so—OK,
yeah, it's not going well," he admitted.

Just then, his cell beeped. Joe glanced at the screen. "It's

Wally." He answered, put the phone to his ear, and listened.

"For real?" he said, his voice rising slightly with excitement. Caitlin clenched and unclenched her fists in anticipation. Joe nodded to her, his eyes alight.

He pocketed the phone. "No time to waste!" he told Caitlin. "Let's go!"

Iris stared at the phone in her hand. "What's up, Iris?" Cisco asked.

They had just spent twenty pointless minutes talking to the second of two people Caitlin could remember being friendly with Earthworm back in his pre-meta days. Nathan Markson was a surgeon now and had precisely no information for them.

"We had a rare night off and got drinks together," the surgeon had said. "That was the day before S.T.A.R. Labs blew up in the town's face. Saw him around the hospital a couple of times later that week but never had a chance to talk with him. Next thing I knew, management had suspended him for not showing up, and then he just dropped off the grid."

And now, as they emerged onto the street, Iris was staring at the phone in her hand. A phone that, Cisco realized, wasn't her own but was, instead, Barry's.

"News?" he asked.

"Frye," she said. "It doesn't look good. His texts are getting more and more cantankerous, and the guy wasn't particularly sweet to begin with."

Cisco sighed. The sky was darkening. The day was already fading into night, and the next afternoon was Barry's disciplinary hearing. So far, Barry had done absolutely nothing to work with his union rep, Darrel Frye, to mount a defense and keep his job. He'd been distracted by Flash-y things, true—Hocus Pocus, Earth 27, the future—but Cisco didn't think the disciplinary board would take that into account. Because they couldn't know that police scientist and sworn upholder of the law Barry Allen was also the vigilante the Flash. A lovable and kind and good-hearted vigilante, to be sure, but a vigilante nonetheless.

"This doesn't look good for Barry's job," Iris said in that tone of voice that meant she wanted Cisco to contradict her.

But he couldn't. He couldn't think of anything to say that was encouraging or uplifting, so he said nothing and felt like a complete heel as Iris did a very good job of not crying. It was an occasion when one good friend would put his arm around another good friend. Cisco was never very good at that sort of thing, but he figured he should start learning now, and just as he lifted his arm, his phone went off.

His arm never did find its way to Iris's shoulder.

His phone beeped. It was Wally.

"You guys shouldn't have left H.R. and me home alone," Wally said when Cisco answered. "We've been up to things."

"Wally, if you touched *any* of the electronics in Lab 4A, there's a chance you're contaminated!" Cisco shouted. "You both need to quarantine yourselves immediately and—"

"Chillax, Cisco! We just did our Herbert Hynde homework. We found his last known address, and when that didn't pan out, we found out where his stuff is stored." Wally paused for a dramatic beat. "I gave the address to Dad, too. Wanna see if you guys can beat him there?"

Iris and Cisco beat Joe and Caitlin to the chain-link fence surrounding the storage facility by less than a minute. They were elated at this small victory on a day that was all about defeats, then crushed when Wally waved to them from inside the fence.

"No fair using superspeed!"

"All's fair in love, war, and tracking bad guys," Wally said, unlocking the gate from the inside. "C'mon. It's storage unit 12F."

As they threaded their way through the maze of low, one-story buildings that made up the storage facility, Wally explained how he'd found Hynde's belongings: He and H.R.

had used the information in the CCGH personnel file to find out where Hynde had been living when he'd gotten his powers. They went to the building, where H.R. used his facial transmogrification device to mimic the appearance of Hynde from his hospital ID badge.

"The landlord was surprised to see him, to say the least," Wally told them. "He said he'd evicted Hynde years ago for not paying his rent, so we figured we'd hit another dead end. But then we got lucky. Turns out the landlord packed up Hynde's stuff and stashed it in a storage unit."

"That's . . . really nice for a landlord," Iris commented.

"'I useta just toss it or sell it off,'" Wally said in an eerily landlord-esque voice. "'But these days you get lawsuits for everything, so . . .'"

"Let's hear it for lawyers and a litigious society," Cisco cracked. "So all of Hynde's stuff is stored here, and we can plunder it for info."

"Plunder?" Joe said. "You sound like a pirate."

"Do *not* say, 'Arr, matey' or anything involving 'Arrr!'" Caitlin warned, much to Cisco's chagrin.

"So, anyway, we, uh, redirected some cash from the S.T.A.R. Labs operating budget to the landlord to pay for back rent and fees, and he told us where the stuff is. H.R.'s holding down the fort back at S.T.A.R."

"Truly, this is the first time in history we've used money to fight crime," Iris marveled.

"Wouldn't it be great if we could just pay off the bad guys?" Caitlin mused aloud.

Cisco opened his mouth to comment, but just then Wally brought them up short. They had turned down a short alley in the maze of storage units. Before them was a squat, square structure with three corrugated doors set into it. The middle one, in faded blue paint, read 12F.

"Earthworm's history!" Wally said. "Abracadabra!"

Cisco shivered. "Never, ever say that again, please."

"Too soon?"

"It will never *not* be too soon."

The door was securely padlocked, but the landlord had given them the key. Joe took it and inserted it into the lock. He grimaced as he turned it, slowly. "This thing is almost completely rusted inside. It hasn't been opened in forever."

Eventually, he was able to get the padlock open. Together, Joe and Wally managed to heave open the door, which rattled and clanked up into the ceiling with a sprinkling of rust.

They peered within. It was getting dark out, the sun setting, and no light came on in the storage unit. Joe produced a flashlight from his coat pocket and played the beam within the confines of the little room.

It was maybe twenty feet by thirty feet but crammed full of boxes and sheet-covered furniture. Cobwebs filled the spaces between boxes, and everything was coated in a layer of dust so thick that it seemed to be solid. The floor was plain asphalt, continued from the alley they'd entered from, sloping gently toward the center of the room.

There was a light switch mounted on the wall just inside the unit, but when Caitlin flicked it, nothing happened.

"Looks like Hynde's landlord economized," Cisco said.

"No heat or A/C for the unit," Joe commented. "No electricity. Nothing to keep rain from coming in under the door . . ."

"Well, he was just trying to keep from getting sued, not win Landlord of the Year," said Wally.

Except for Joe, who already had a flashlight, everyone else dug out their cell phones and switched on the lights. The unit lit up a bit, but the haphazard arrangement of furniture and the stacks of boxes threw out scads of shadows in every direction.

"Let's get our hands dirty," Joe said, and he stepped inside. The others followed.

There wasn't much elbow room in the unit. The light spilling in from outside was weak, but at least it supplemented their phones. They huddled together. Cisco sneezed mightily at the profusion of dust.

"We're not gonna be able to find anything in here," he complained.

"Hang on," Wally said. "Look."

There was a little open space between two piles of boxes. He was the smallest, so he squeezed through it, the towers on either side of him swaying dangerously.

"Don't knock anything over!" Joe warned him.

"I'm Kid Flash! I'll be fine!"

"I'm worried about *evidence*."

"Your concern is touching, Dad," Wally called back, his voice fading as he moved farther into the forest of boxes.

Joe snorted and nudged aside a box, peering deeper into the storage unit. "I think I see something up ahead."

With Cisco, he pressed farther in. The floor sloped a bit more here; Joe played his light down at his feet and saw a grate set into the floor. Cheap storage unit. Rather than have waterproofing around the doors, just put in a sewer drain and let the water run on in and then run on down and out.

Meanwhile, Iris and Caitlin had stripped a sheet away from a large lump off to the left of the door. It turned out to be a gray-green futon that had seen better days. They both pinched their noses at the mildew odor that erupted from it and looked at each other.

"Definitely a boy's furniture," Caitlin said.

"You should have seen the easy chair I made Barry throw out," Iris said. "Ugh."

At the same time, Wally was prowling through a stack of plastic tubs stacked high atop one another. They were barely translucent, and he could just make out endless piles of books within.

"Anyone find anything?" he called out. A chorus of "No!" came back to him from various points in the storage unit, so he kept pawing around.

Meanwhile, Joe and Cisco pushed aside a set of cheap, stacked dining room chairs and found a smallish pressboard desk. *Desk* was actually a strong word—it had four legs and a warped surface atop them, along with a busted drawer that hung partly out of its socket. It resembled a desk, but calling it one was being charitable.

On the rickety top was an older-model laptop trailing a power cable. Connected to the laptop was a small external hard drive.

"Wait a sec." Joe stopped Cisco from moving forward. "This doesn't make any sense. Why pack up everything else, but just chuck the guy's computer onto a piece of furniture and leave it here?"

Cisco shrugged off Joe's hand and advanced. "Who cares?" He lifted the laptop and was surprised when the screen lit up right away. He followed the cable with his eyes: It snaked to the floor, then up the wall and into the ceiling.

"Oho! I see!" Cisco pointed up. "This is why the overhead light didn't work. Someone spliced into the wiring and rerouted it to the computer."

Joe grabbed Cisco by his elbow and pulled him back. "Don't be an idiot, Cisco! You know what this means! Someone's been in here. Someone's using this stuff."

Even as he said it, Joe's spine crawled with cold tentacles. He remembered the sewer drain set into the middle of the sloping floor. "Oh, no . . ." he said.

Suddenly, there was a creak and a rattle from overhead. The door! It was moving!

Before anyone could react, the door slammed shut, trapping them inside the storage unit.

The little room was utterly dark, save for the spots of illumination from cell phones and Joe's flashlight. It wasn't *much* darker than it had been before, but the closing of the door made it feel so.

"There's someone in here!" Caitlin shouted from close to the entrance. She and Iris immediately stood back-to-back.

"Ya *think*?" Cisco cried.

"Guys, chill!" Wally called from somewhere else. "Don't panic!"

"Who's panicking?" Cisco demanded, panicked.

"Wait!" Joe this time. "Hear that?"

"Hear what?" Iris asked, her back pressed to Caitlin's.

They all fell silent for a moment. From somewhere distant came the sound of . . . chittering. And the minute click of paws on asphalt.

"Oh, no!" Wally yelled. "Not again!"

Cisco felt something brush against his leg. He jerked back instinctively and shrieked in a high falsetto when he looked down to see an enormous rat running past him.

"OH MY GOD!" he screamed.

Joe spun around, his pistol drawn and elevated. "Everyone go quiet!" he commanded. "Keep your lights on!"

Caitlin stomped down with her heel as hard as she could and felt a sickening crunch beneath her foot. She swallowed hard, stifling the urge to vomit. Behind her, Iris sucked in her breath and then did the same, crushing another rat with her foot.

"It's crawling up my leg!" Cisco howled in the darkness.

"Look up!" Wally yelled. "Look up!"

Iris wanted to look down because the idea of a rat getting close enough to climb up *her* leg had her heart pumping like a firefighter in front of a ten-alarm blaze. But if Wally was saying, *Look up* . . .

She aimed her phone up. There, on the ceiling, she

caught a glimpse of something yellow, trailing bedraggled, threadbare black cloth.

Earthworm! Oh my God, it's him! Right here!

"Holy—!" Caitlin gasped, and Iris knew she'd seen him, too.

"He's gone!" Iris exclaimed. "So fast—!"

And then she jerked her leg back and kicked, connecting solidly with another rat.

Wally winced as gunshots echoed loudly in the confines of the storage space. His dad was trying to shoot down Earthworm, which Wally knew was pointless. The villain moved like a shadow, like oil on water. A gun in the dark was no good against him. From bitter experience, Wally knew that they'd have to think their way around Hynde.

"Stop shooting!" he yelled, but he could barely hear himself over the din of the gunshots echoing in the confined space. He put his hands over his ears, trying to block out the noise and the knowledge that the rats would soon be on him, trying to *think* . . .

And that's when he saw . . .

Joe emptied his clip at the ceiling and received only a ringing in his ears, a patchy drift of gun smoke, and the smell of cordite in return. If he'd hit anything other than the joists overhead, he'd be amazed.

He and Cisco had backed up to a wall. Cisco had recovered enough from his initial shock to use his vibe powers to keep the rats away, but he was still new to the powers, and it wasn't something he could keep up forever.

Fumbling to slide a fresh clip into his gun, Joe tried to force himself not to think of Iris, not far from him but far enough, with a legion of rats sinking their teeth into her ankles, crawling through her hair . . .

Sweat dripped down Cisco's forehead and into his eyes, but he didn't dare blink to clear them. He was trying something different: Instead of focusing his vibe energy in a single, intense, instantaneous blast, he was letting it flow out of him in a slow, continuous flux, fanning it out into an arc. It had less potency along its length but had greater overall area, holding off more rats at once.

He couldn't keep it up forever, though. No one could. Someone had to do something. *Fast.*

Overhead, there was a hiss. Cisco didn't dare look up, but he heard Joe suck in his breath in shock, then raise his gun again. Cisco braced himself for the pounding of the gunshots against his ears.

"Upworlders," a voice hissed. "Soon to be no more. Good-bye . . ."

Joe fired ten rapid shots. Cisco momentarily lost control

of his vibe, and a rat slipped through. He shook it off his leg and refocused on the vibe.

Wally blinked. Unlike Barry, he wasn't an expert in munitions and explosives, but he was pretty sure he knew a bomb when one was right in front of him.

Like, say, right now.

Sitting on a slightly tilted crate before him was a block of grayish putty that he was sure was C-4 explosive compound. At some point in the past, Barry had told him that C-4 was a combination of explosive, plasticizer, rubber, and mineral oil, and also that it was completely stable by itself—you needed a shock-wave detonation to set it off.

There was a black stick poking out of the C-4, which Wally was pretty sure was the detonator. And a set of twisting wires going from the detonator to the faceplate of a digital clock, which was counting down from—three seconds.

Well, make that *two* seconds now.

"Cisco!" Wally screamed at the top of his lungs. "You gotta—"

A moment later, the bomb went off, and the storage unit erupted, filling with fire and light and the thunderous crashing sound of an explosion.

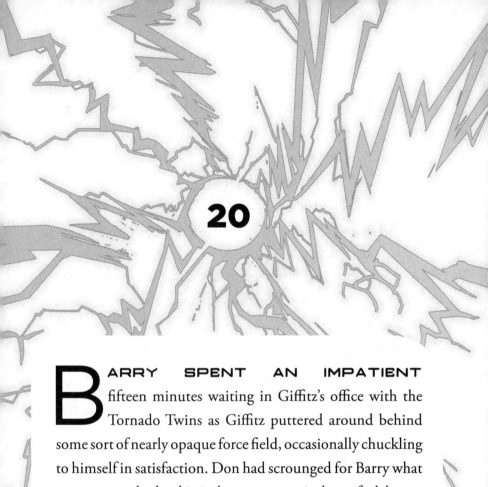

20

BARRY SPENT AN IMPATIENT fifteen minutes waiting in Giffitz's office with the Tornado Twins as Giffitz puttered around behind some sort of nearly opaque force field, occasionally chuckling to himself in satisfaction. Don had scrounged for Barry what was apparently the thirtieth-century equivalent of a lab coat from a locker; it was bright blue, nearly skintight, and had a flaring collar and enormous epaulets. It felt ridiculous, but he reminded himself: When in Rome . . . or in the future . . .

Maybe this is why Eobard Thawne went nuts, he thought. *Having to wear crazy futuristic clothes.*

The twins made excited conversation with him while they waited, asking questions about his twenty-first century life and especially about his relationship with Iris. It was just starting to get uncomfortably personal when Giffitz emerged from his work space with the costume. It was all in one piece again and looked shiny and new. It was also a much brighter shade of red and somewhat less bulky.

"Thanks," Barry said, taking it. "Now we—"

"Wait, wait." Giffitz shook a finger in a *hang on* gesture. "Your ring. Open it."

Barry shrugged and twisted open the top of the lightning ring. In less than the blink of an eye and with a soft *sssssh* sound the costume in his hands vanished, shrinking and suddenly being sucked right into the ring.

"Wow!" Despite himself and despite the urgency of his situation, Barry couldn't help but be impressed. "How did you do that?"

Giffitz shrugged. "Your ring is a standard model collapsing storage system. Invented about five hundred years ago and based on some ancient Palmertech. Very old, very reliable, and stable technology. All I did was treat your costume to be compatible with it."

Barry stared down at the ring, which had closed itself automatically once the costume was inside. The scientist in him had to know: "How does it work?"

"The material of your costume has been impregnated with a chemical that reacts to nitrogen; hence, the change in color. In the absence of nitrogen, the molecules of the costume contract, shrinking down so that it will fit in the ring. The ring itself strips away nitrogen when it's empty."

Barry nodded. He got it. Nitrogen was common in the atmosphere. In fact, most people thought of oxygen when they thought of the air they breathed, but nitrogen made up almost eighty percent of the earth's atmosphere. Oxygen was only about twenty percent.

"When I open the ring with the costume in it," Barry said, "the presence of nitrogen causes the costume to expand. When I open it empty, it sucks the nitrogen out of the costume, shrinking it." He stared down at the ring admiringly. "Awesome."

Giffitz harrumphed. "Hardly, young man. Extremely basic and—as I said before—old-fashioned technology. A child could do it."

Barry opened his mouth to tell Giffitz that maybe the man needed to consider someone else's perspective, but at that moment, the building shook, then kept on shaking, as though something enormous were pounding it.

Earthquake! was Barry's first thought, but then he remembered: The entire building was suspended in midair. A massive earthquake could rip a fault line open right below them, and the building wouldn't budge an inch.

Giffitz staggered with the ongoing tremors, stumbling across the room as a floating desk bounced off a wall and careened toward him. Barry zipped over at superspeed and pulled Giffitz out of harm's way.

"What's going on?" he shouted.

Dawn rushed to a wall. Where she touched it, it went transparent, revealing the sprawl of buildings outside. Now he understood why there were no windows. The buildings were all fabricated from some kind of polarized substance or alloy. There could be a window wherever you wanted or needed one.

"What's going on here?" Barry asked her. "Did something hit us? Is the building stable?"

Dawn squinted, peering out onto the campus.

"Oh," she said after a moment. "It looks like we're under attack by space pirates."

There was a protracted moment of silence, during which the building shook again. "Space pirates?" Barry said at last.

"It happens a lot these days," Dawn admitted. "No one's really sure why."

The building shook again.

"We have to hold tight until the Science Police get here," Don said. "They have to scramble from the Weisinger Plaza precinct. Should only take them about five minutes to get here."

Barry stared through the "window." Hovering over the city's fusion powersphere was a large vessel that looked something like a submarine with gigantic fins. As he watched, bolts of sizzling blue energy shot out of the vessel and slammed into buildings and the ground. Everything shook.

"ATTENTION, EARTH IDIOTS!" a voice rang out. "I AM ROXXAS, AND YOU ARE NOW MY PRISONERS!"

"Roxxas!" Don whistled. "Last I heard, he was headed for Trom. Wonder what brought him back to Earth."

Dawn considered. "I heard the Brande gate near Alpha Centauri is glitchy. Maybe he decided to stick around here."

"Guys!" Barry snapped his fingers to get their attention. "Focus, please. People could be getting hurt down there, and you said it'll take the cops at least five minutes to get here."

Don and Dawn exchanged a twin-look, then looked at him. "What can we do? We can't fly up there and stop his ship from attacking."

Barry fumed. He turned back to the window, scanning the situation. In an instant, the solution occurred to him. But he couldn't do it alone.

"C'mon," he told the Tornado Twins. "I'm deputizing you into the superhero club."

The three of them abandoned the university building and hit the ground running. Literally.

Barry had given the twins their marching—well, *running*—orders: Protect civilians. Scour the area at super-speed and help anyone in trouble. Don and Dawn had rushed off, both of them flushed with excitement and a little bit of fear.

Before they left, though, they asked him: "What about Roxxas?"

"I'll handle Roxxas," Barry said confidently, and he ran off to do just that.

The twins had told him that it was illegal to run on top of the fusion powersphere. Barry had great respect for the law, but these were extreme circumstances. He ran around the powersphere a couple of times to build up momentum, then ran up its slope.

It was sort of slippery, and his feet seemed to crackle where they touched the surface. He knew that fusion power was safe, but it still unnerved him. He hoped he wasn't doing any damage to himself by getting so close.

Oh, well. No one could live forever, right?

He ran up the powersphere until he was at its top, where he ran around and around in a circle until he'd built up the appropriate amount of speed. And then . . .

He flung himself headlong into the sky, right at Roxxas's spaceship. The thing had looked pretty small from the ground, but now that he got closer, it was massive. One of those blue bolts of energy crisped the air nearby, its heat and force nearly throwing Barry off course.

At the last possible second, he vibrated his molecules, slipping through the molecular structure of the ship and emerging inside. A group of motley-looking aliens and humans gasped in surprise. They all reached for weapons, but they stood no chance. The Flash disarmed them all in less than a second and knocked them out cold.

Except for one.

"Where's Roxxas?" Barry demanded. The only conscious pirate was a blue-skinned guy who looked to be in his late teens. All his bluster and bravado had vanished along with the weird futuristic gun Barry had snatched from him at superspeed.

"Through there!" the guy cried, pointing to what Barry imagined was a door. "On the bridge!"

Barry shook the pirate into unconsciousness and vibrated through the door. No time to figure out how to open it.

On the other side was a little less Starship *Enterprise* than he'd expected. The bridge was cramped and dirty, with just enough room for a large command chair and two support stations. Barry took out the aliens at the support stations first, then spun around to confront Roxxas himself.

Like the rest of the thirtieth century, he was a fashion disaster: skintight gray pants, blue boots that came to the knee and flared, a black shirt that was open all the way down to his navel. He had a wickedly sharp mustache and a pointy little goatee, both of which reminded Barry—with a shiver—of Hocus Pocus.

"Your pirating days are over," Barry told him.

Roxxas looked him up and down. "Who in the Nebula do you think *you*—"

He never finished the sentence. Barry yanked him out of his control chair and threw him to the floor. "I don't have time to figure out your controls. Set a course off this planet, and don't come back, got it?"

Roxxas snarled and reached for a weapon clipped to his belt, but by the time his hand got there, the weapon was gone. Barry juggled it for the pirate's benefit, enjoying the look of shock on the man's face.

"I . . . think I'll go elsewhere," Roxxas said with a gulp.

"Good call. Earth's off-limits. Got it?"

"Got it."

As the pirate scrambled back to his control chair, Barry vibrated through the deck of the ship, then went into free fall above the city. He had planned well, though: He dropped right back onto the apex of the fusion powersphere and ran down its curvature to the ground.

Looking up, he shaded his eyes against the setting sun

and watched as Roxxas's ship turned and blasted off over the horizon and into outer space.

The Tornado Twins screeched to identical halts at his side. "Wow!" Dawn breathed. "You did it! You got him to leave!"

"Casualties?" Barry asked.

"None," Don told him. "We were fast enough. No one's hurt."

Barry nodded. "Good. Look, kids, this has been fun, but it's time for me to go. No pun intended."

The Tornado Twins sighed at exactly the same moment for exactly the same length of time. "Yeah, we know," Dawn said with a note of sad resignation in her voice. "C'mon. We'll get you to the future."

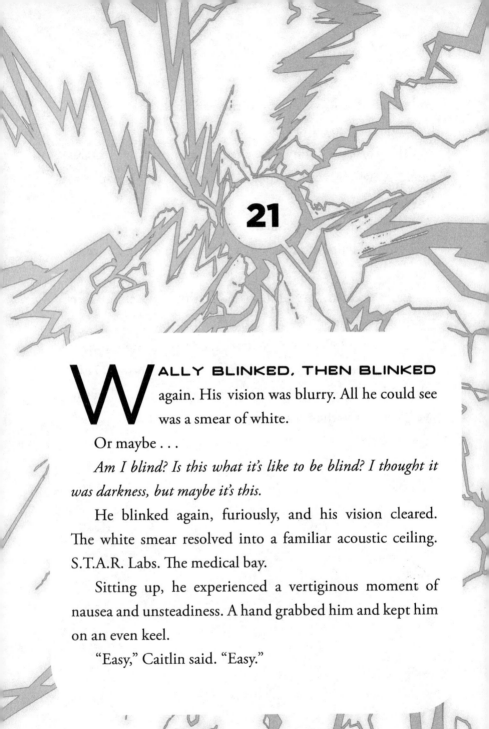

21

WALLY BLINKED, THEN BLINKED again. His vision was blurry. All he could see was a smear of white.

Or maybe . . .

Am I blind? Is this what it's like to be blind? I thought it was darkness, but maybe it's this.

He blinked again, furiously, and his vision cleared. The white smear resolved into a familiar acoustic ceiling. S.T.A.R. Labs. The medical bay.

Sitting up, he experienced a vertiginous moment of nausea and unsteadiness. A hand grabbed him and kept him on an even keel.

"Easy," Caitlin said. "Easy."

Wally looked around. Caitlin stood to his right, one hand holding a portable medical scanner, the other helping to keep him upright. Iris sat on the other side of the bed and took his left hand in both of hers.

"If anyone ever doubted Kid Flash was a hero," she said, "those doubts are cleared away for good."

"What happened?" he asked. "I just remember the bomb . . ."

"You saved us," Caitlin said. "You and Cisco, really, but it was your idea and quick thinking."

Wally almost couldn't believe it. He'd saved a lot of people since becoming Kid Flash—it was pretty awesome, saving people—but the idea that *he* had managed to foil a super villain's plot and save his friends and family? The idea that he'd beaten Earthworm, at least temporarily?

And then it started to come back to him. He remembered seeing the bomb. The timer. Three seconds left. And then two . . .

Two seconds was a ridiculously long time for Kid Flash. But it wasn't only Kid Flash who was needed for this rescue. Just finding everyone in the darkened tumult of the storage unit would eat up a second, maybe a little more. That didn't leave enough time to phase everyone through the door and far enough away to be safe.

So Wally burned three-tenths of a second thinking of a better way and realized he would need Cisco. He'd shouted:

"Cisco! You gotta open a breach!"

Now saving everyone was a manageable task. He didn't need to sweep up Cisco and Joe; he just had to find his sister and Caitlin and get them to Cisco. Hopefully, Cisco had heard him, had understood, and had opened the breach already.

He dashed back along the route he'd taken to the bomb in the first place, now not caring if he jostled things out of position or sent boxes crashing down around one another. This whole place was going to be ash and fire and debris in a few seconds, anyway.

He stepped over, around, and—once or twice—on rats along the way, the furry little knife-toothed beasts frozen in his path. Caitlin and Iris were right in front of him when he emerged from the boxes, standing back-to-back as Joe had taught them to do in crisis situations. Made it tougher for bad guys to sneak up on you.

When the "bad guys" were a billion rats, though, it was less helpful. Wally plucked a rat from Iris's hair, tossing it over his shoulder. When he turned to watch it spiral off into the darkness, he noticed a burgeoning yellow-gold light behind him.

The bomb had gone off. He figured he had maybe a second and a half before it engulfed the storage unit. Rat patrol would have to wait.

He grabbed Caitlin and Iris by their wrists and ran. It wasn't the most delicate way to handle things, but desperate times called for desperate measures.

On the ceiling, he could see a flashlight beam, calcified and pinned to the roof. Bullet holes glimmered there, still steaming with impact heat. That was where his father and Cisco had to be. Right under there.

Cisco, if you didn't open a breach, they're not gonna be able to peel what's left of us off a wall.

He raced ahead. Off to his right, the blossom of the explosion was nearly in full flower. Heat and smoke and ash burst forth at him. Tightening his grip on Caitlin and Iris, he ran forward, shouldering aside boxes and crates. Assuming they survived, Caitlin and Iris would probably have serious bruises on their wrists and quite possibly dislocated shoulders, but he figured they'd prefer that to the alternative of being blown to smithereens. His own shoulders were already aching with the strain of dragging two full-grown adults behind him.

Ahead, he saw his dad and Cisco, and right behind them was a beautiful, gorgeous, coruscating whirl of blurry, distorted light. A breach. Cisco had heard.

Wally plowed straight ahead without hesitation. He bodychecked his father, knocking him into Cisco, the two of them tumbling into the breach as Wally, with the last of his strength, swung his arms forward and used his momentum to shove Iris and Caitlin into the breach, as well.

The explosion was all around him now. He heard its heat sizzling the ends of his hair. His back was smoldering. He didn't think he would make it to the breach himself, but at least he'd saved everyone else . . .

"I made it," Wally said in wonderment. "We all made it."

"Thanks to you." Iris patted him on the arm. "Caitlin says you—"

"Caitlin says you have some minor burns on your back and shoulders," Caitlin interrupted, "but nothing your speedster metabolism won't quickly heal." She dropped the hand holding her medical scanner to her side and smiled broadly at him. "Thanks, Wally. Good job."

Wally leaned back against his pillow. His satisfaction fled as quickly as he'd gotten everyone out of the storage unit. "Good job? I guess. But we lost all the evidence. If I'd seen the bomb sooner or been just a little bit faster . . ."

Iris chuckled. "Does the guilt complex come with the superspeed, or was it there all along? With you and Barry, I'm never sure."

"He must have had a motion sensor on the door," Wally said. "So he'd know if anyone broke into his place. And then he came up through the sewer . . . to make sure we'd never get any clues."

"Well, he failed at that," Caitlin told him. At his surprised expression, she crooked a finger at him. "C'mon. As your doctor, I'm pronouncing you in good-enough health to get up and walk to the Cortex."

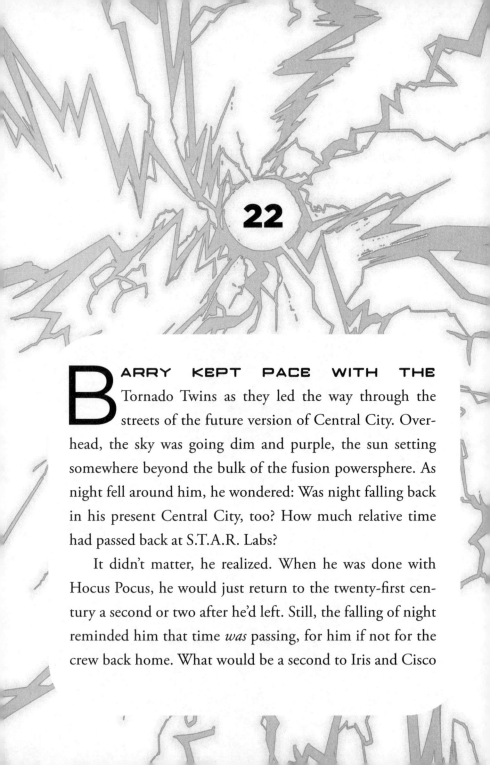

22

BARRY KEPT PACE WITH THE Tornado Twins as they led the way through the streets of the future version of Central City. Overhead, the sky was going dim and purple, the sun setting somewhere beyond the bulk of the fusion powersphere. As night fell around him, he wondered: Was night falling back in his present Central City, too? How much relative time had passed back at S.T.A.R. Labs?

It didn't matter, he realized. When he was done with Hocus Pocus, he would just return to the twenty-first century a second or two after he'd left. Still, the falling of night reminded him that time *was* passing, for him if not for the crew back home. What would be a second to Iris and Cisco and the others was already a few hours to him. He yearned to be done with all this time travel business and get back to what passed for normal.

Don cut left and phased through a wall. Dawn followed, and Barry joined them. He found himself inside a dark alcove with the twins.

"Now what?" he asked.

"Security?" Don asked Dawn.

Dawn shrugged and touched the wall closest to her. A holographic interface lit up there. She tapped a few glowing pads and dragged a slider from one extreme to another. Somewhere outside the alcove, lights came on.

"Uh, guys? Are we doing anything illegal here?" Barry asked. The tech was futuristic, but anyone could tell that Dawn had just disabled some kind of security system. As the Flash, Barry indulged in vigilante justice, which, technically, was against the law, but he'd convinced himself that as long as he remained within certain parameters, he was doing more good than bad.

Breaking and entering—even in a future long after he would be dead and buried—crossed a line.

"Nah," Don said. "Our, uh, family contributes here. We're allowed in when it's closed."

Barry thought he was a pretty good judge of character;

he didn't think Don was lying, and so far the twins hadn't steered him wrong. He left the alcove, peered around a corridor, and turned to his left.

"Nope," Don said, grabbing him by the elbow. "This way." He guided Barry to the right.

At the end of the corridor, a door opened at Dawn's command. Beyond lay an expansive, dimly lit chamber with paths among large floating display cases.

"What is this place?" Barry asked as they wended their way through the chamber.

"It's sort of a museum," Dawn said.

That made sense. Everything he saw seemed preserved like an exhibit, right down to floating holographic "plaques" written in a language he couldn't decipher. The telepathic earplug Dawn had lent him could translate speech but not the written word, apparently.

Some of the items looked familiar, which was weird. There was, for example, a S.T.A.R. Labs baseball cap of all things, perfectly preserved and resting on a cushion in a glass case. Near that, he spied a ragged, yellowed front page of the *Central City Picture News*, mounted and hovering. He didn't need to read the plaque for this one. The newspaper was in good old twenty-first-century English and read: WHO IS THE STREAK? One of the very first media mentions of the

Flash, before anyone knew who or what he was or what he looked like.

"What kind of museum?" he asked. It seemed specifically geared toward his own time period.

"What we're looking for is through here," Dawn said, pointing.

"I want to check out more of this stuff," Barry told her.

"Aren't you the one who's in a hurry to get to the sixty-fourth century?" Don asked.

Good point. Barry turned away from another display—what appeared to be a scale model of S.T.A.R. Labs itself—and followed the twins into another room.

This one was much smaller. And even though he couldn't read the Interlac holographic signage drifting around, he didn't need to know the exact words to understand the intent: The signs glowed a red that said *Danger! Don't touch anything!*

In the center of the room was a contraption that looked something like a conveyor belt with two sleek, shiny posts jutting up from one side, supporting a slender control panel. The more he stared at it, the more he thought it almost looked like a mutant treadmill, with a wide belt to run on and the controls on the side instead of in front.

Dawn confirmed his suspicions an instant later. She gestured to the device and said, "Ta-da! The Cosmic Treadmill!"

Barry smirked. "That's the kind of name my buddy Cisco would come up with."

Don chuckled. "It's your path straight to the sixty-fourth century. No muss, no fuss."

"Really?" Barry paced around the Treadmill, occasionally walking through one of the holographic warning signs. "It doesn't look like much. How does it work?"

Dawn came up beside him. "You set your destination time on the control panel. The Treadmill does all the work of figuring out speed vectors and stuff like that. All you have to do is run, and it takes the energy from your velocity and adjusts your internal vibrations for you. Sends you right to where—"

"When," Don interrupted.

She stuck her tongue out at her brother. "Fine. Sends you right to *when* you want to go."

Barry rocked back on his heels. That sounded a *lot* easier than the method he'd used to get this far. "So you don't need to work up to light speed?"

"No need. The Treadmill channels energy straight from the Speed Force for you, modifies your internal vibrations, and automatically cuts the energy feed when you've arrived at the right period."

With a frown, Barry crouched, peering at the running belt. "It sounds too easy. If time travel were this simple, everyone would be doing it."

"Well, you have to have superspeed in the first place to activate the chronometric circuits," Dawn told him. "Otherwise, you can run on it forever and get nowhere."

"Like any normal treadmill," Don said.

Barry extended his hand and lightly touched the Treadmill. *I don't know what I was expecting. It doesn't feel like anything special.*

"This isn't the original," Dawn said with a note of regret. "That one isn't functional anymore. It's somewhere in the museum's warehouse, boxed up with some other stuff."

"But this is a fully functional re-creation, with shock absorbers forged out of maganium inertron," Don told him. "It'll get you to the sixty-fourth century, no problem."

"And then, to get home, you just relax your internal vibrations and *zip!* You're back in the twenty-first century!" Dawn smiled broadly. "Simple!"

With a nod and a small grin, Barry agreed. Yeah, sure. Simple. None of this was simple by any definition, but at least it all seemed possible.

"All right," he said. "Let's set the destination time for the sixty-fourth century and see how this puppy works."

Cisco's "reverse carbon-dating" idea had pegged the wand as coming from the year 6345, sometime in the middle of that year. The Treadmill's interface was in Interlac, so Barry had the twins set it for him.

"Hocus Pocus came to my time in late September," Barry told them, and then gave them the exact date. "Let's assume that he traveled back from the same date in his own time."

Dawn agreed. "Most time travelers try to do that. If you leave for the past on, say, December 1, it makes sense to arrive in the past on December 1 in whatever year you're aiming for. It keeps the numbers even and makes it easier to remember when you left and when you arrived. Unless there's a specific reason to go to another day."

"He was just in town to cause havoc," Barry said. "No reason to aim for a specific day or time. At least, I don't think so."

"It should be close enough." Don started tapping on the control panel. "We'll add in a few days from his departure to take into account how long he was in the twenty-first century before he escaped from your Pipeline. You should arrive in 6345 the same day he got back."

"Perfect." Barry licked his lips as Don stepped back. The twins stood off to one side and watched expectantly. They were so antsy that Barry thought there should be a drumroll as he stepped up onto the Treadmill.

"So, I just run?" he asked.

"Yep." Dawn clenched her hands together as if praying. Barry hoped it wasn't for him.

He grabbed the side bar and stretched briefly, then started to run.

The effect of the Treadmill hit him immediately. Unlike speeding around the particle accelerator, drafting off Wally's speed, the impact was instantaneous and almost effortless. The coruscating, multihued tunnel of the time stream appeared before him instantly. In the next moment, it was all around him; the Tornado Twins and the room at the museum vanished as the colors of time itself spun around him.

He looked down. There was nothing there, but he could swear he still felt the belt of the Treadmill beneath his feet.

Effortlessly, the Flash ran to the future.

The Tornado Twins watched as the Flash vanished before their eyes. For several long, silent seconds, they simply stood there, holding hands, gazing at the spot on the Cosmic Treadmill where Barry Allen had been running mere moments before.

At last, Don spoke: "⊓ᒪ▽ᒪ! ⊓⑂ ⊐ᗺ⑂▽⊐ᒪᒪ⌂ ▽◔⊐⏚ᖴ◌!"

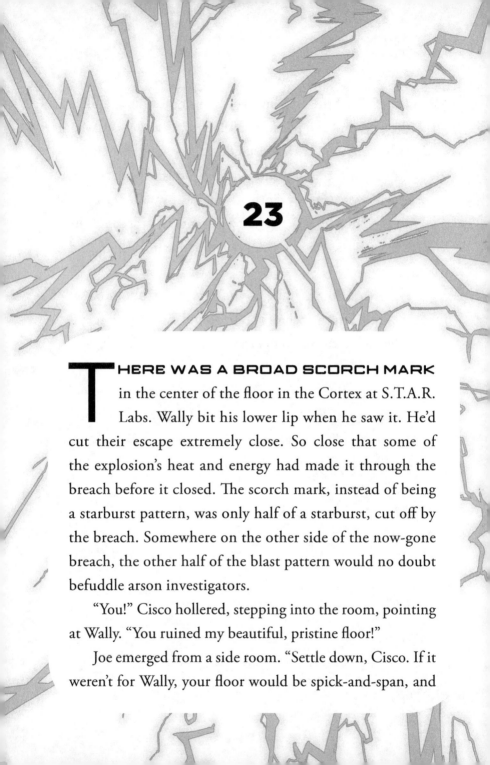

23

THERE WAS A BROAD SCORCH MARK in the center of the floor in the Cortex at S.T.A.R. Labs. Wally bit his lower lip when he saw it. He'd cut their escape extremely close. So close that some of the explosion's heat and energy had made it through the breach before it closed. The scorch mark, instead of being a starburst pattern, was only half of a starburst, cut off by the breach. Somewhere on the other side of the now-gone breach, the other half of the blast pattern would no doubt befuddle arson investigators.

"You!" Cisco hollered, stepping into the room, pointing at Wally. "You ruined my beautiful, pristine floor!"

Joe emerged from a side room. "Settle down, Cisco. If it weren't for Wally, your floor would be spick-and-span, and your body would be charred pulp spread out over a ten-foot radius in storage unit 12F."

"Yeah. Like, you're welcome for saving your life and stuff," Wally told Cisco.

"Life, schmife." Cisco produced a plastic-coated rubber band from his pocket and shook his head to toss his hair back and forth. "The explosion singed the ends of my gorgeous locks. I've cultivated this waterfall of ebon tresses for years, Kid Flash. Now I have to—*ugh!*—go pony." He gathered his long hair in a fist and slipped the rubber band over it. Then he quickly checked his reflection in one of the many window-walls in the Cortex.

"Actually, that looks amazing!" he marveled, stroking the hair at his temples. "I guess when you're this pretty, there's not much that can ruin your looks."

"If we can end the hair-care commercial," Iris said, "and move on . . . ?"

"Was anyone else nearby hurt in the explosion?" Wally asked.

"No, we were the only ones in the danger zone," Caitlin informed him.

"Central City's Bravest were on the scene in three minutes," Joe announced. "Had the fire contained and out within an hour." He shook his head. "Firefighters are crazy," he said to no one in particular.

"Caitlin said Earthworm failed at getting rid of all of the clues. What's up?" Wally asked.

"I'm glad you asked," Cisco said. "What took you so long? Ta-da!" He swooped his hand down over a nearby desk and came up with a rounded rectangular solid cast in silver. It had ports cut into it. *Hard drive*, Wally realized. An external hard drive.

"Earthworm's backup drive," Cisco announced. "I grabbed it off his sad excuse for a desk right before the fire and the jumpy guy on the ceiling and the"—he shuddered—"rats."

Wally shuddered, too, in empathetic memory. He knew a woman at school who kept a rat as a pet. He'd never be able to look at that rat the same way again.

"He was actively using the computer, so this backup should be relatively recent," Cisco said. "Let's dive in, shall we?"

Poring through the contents of Earthworm's hard drive took longer than expected. It was a big drive, packed with data going back ten years, to Herbert Hynde's days in medical school. Some kind of glitch had removed most of the created-by dates from the files, so Cisco, Wally, Iris, and Caitlin divvied them up and went through them manually. Joe had a late shift at the precinct but promised to come back when he could. H.R. pled ignorance of primitive Earth 1 computers but did an excellent job keeping them optimally caffeinated for the task at hand.

Eventually, they began to piece together what had happened.

"Poor Herbie," Caitlin murmured.

She read a journal entry dated the day after the particle accelerator explosion:

Still feel a bit flu-ish, but I can't miss a shift. I'll see if someone can give me a flu shot and maybe hook myself up to an IV to keep hydrated.

Saw a man today on my ER shift named Cameron Scott. His skin had developed patches of a silvery eczema. Eczema is probably the wrong word—it wasn't bumpy or uneven. It was smooth and seemed to conform to the contours of his skin. None of us had ever seen anything like it. We admitted him for observation. Wish we could do more.

An entry from a day later:

Actually studied myself in the mirror this morning. Thought it was the lighting in my apartment, but my skin seems yellowish. Looks the same under the lights in the hospital, and a nurse even commented on it.

Could it be jaundice? I don't have any other symptoms—no itching or nausea, though I still feel under the weather. Weird.

And a day after that:

Skin seems a deeper yellow now. Going to run a liver-enzyme test at the hospital today. Also, check my bilirubin levels and do a blood panel, just to be safe. Had weird dreams.

Personal note: My hair is thinning even more. Found a clump in the sink when I washed my face. Great.

"It's like watching a horror movie in slow motion," Cisco said. "Where you know the ending already, but *he* doesn't."

Caitlin shook her head and worried her bottom lip. "He had no idea what was coming."

Wally found an entry from several weeks later. By now, Hynde was no longer going to the hospital. His journal had become scattered and somewhat stream-of-consciousness. Difficult to interpret.

"It's a bunch of numbers and letters," Wally said. "Gibberish."

"Let me look at it." Caitlin peered over his shoulder.

Iris stood up abruptly. "I'll be right back."

She disappeared into the hallway, then took a turn and stepped into an alcove. Once there, she pulled Barry's phone out of her pocket. It had vibrated insistently at her, and she knew why.

"Hello, Mr. Frye," she said, answering.

"Let me guess: Allen isn't available right now."

Iris sighed heavily. Every fiber of her being wanted to be able to answer that question differently. "Well, no," she replied.

"It's nine at night," Frye grumped. "His hearing is in fifteen hours. He can call me at any point during those fifteen hours if he decides to take this seriously. I'll be at the hearing at noon sharp. If he isn't there, well, make sure he understands there's not much I can do. By which I mean: There's absolutely nothing—zero, zilch, nil, nada—that I can do."

"I'll tell him," Iris whispered, then rubbed fiercely at the tears that sprang up at the corners of her eyes. Right now, she would be thrilled just to see Barry again, never mind help him keep his beloved job. Earthworm was a good distraction, such that she'd managed to not think of Barry lost in the time stream for a whole day, but it was a fact: He was gone. If Darrel Frye knew why Barry hadn't called him back, maybe the man would soften. But Iris sort of doubted it. Frye didn't seem like the kind of man who softened for anything.

"When I see him, I'll tell him," she said as steadily as she could, but when Frye broke the connection, she allowed herself to weep silently there in the alcove.

Come back, Barry. Wherever you are, whenever you are, please, please, please come back.

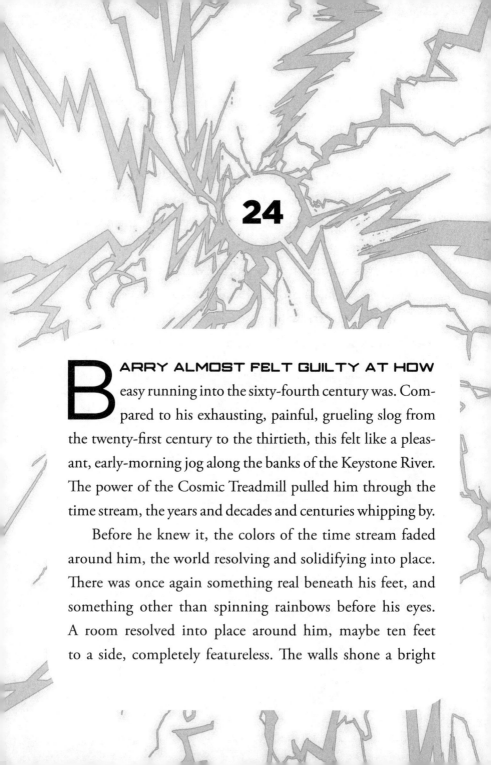

24

BARRY ALMOST FELT GUILTY AT HOW easy running into the sixty-fourth century was. Compared to his exhausting, painful, grueling slog from the twenty-first century to the thirtieth, this felt like a pleasant, early-morning jog along the banks of the Keystone River. The power of the Cosmic Treadmill pulled him through the time stream, the years and decades and centuries whipping by.

Before he knew it, the colors of the time stream faded around him, the world resolving and solidifying into place. There was once again something real beneath his feet, and something other than spinning rainbows before his eyes. A room resolved into place around him, maybe ten feet to a side, completely featureless. The walls shone a bright white, as did the ceiling and floor. He felt as though he'd materialized into a commercial for a new smartphone.

There was a woman standing right in front of him, patiently waiting as though she'd been expecting him. She wore a blue and silver jumpsuit with a shining white helmet that had a clear face shield. She smiled at Barry, inclined her head in greeting, and spoke:

"✋ ⚡ 📅 ⑥ ③ ④ ⑤"

Barry blinked and put one hand up to his ear. Sure enough, the telepathic plug that Dawn had lent him was still there. Had it been damaged by the rigors of time travel?

"👉 👌?" the woman said. "🖼 😕 ?"

"I don't understand you," Barry told her. "I don't think my telepathic plug is working anymore."

The woman stared for a moment, her expression blank, and then her eyes widened in understanding. She raised a finger, and a part of Barry was charmed and relieved to notice that even millennia into the future, the gesture for *Hang on a second* hadn't changed.

She fiddled with her helmet for a moment, then nodded once. Her eyes closed, then opened again, and she smiled and said, "Is this better?"

Exhaling a sigh of relief, Barry said, "Yes! Much! I think my telepathic plug must be on the fritz."

"It's been automatically disabled by our citywide electromagnetic targeting system," the woman said. "Telepathy is illegal in this era, so we can't allow such technology to function."

"Then how are we understanding each other right now?"

She tapped her helmet. "I downloaded standard American English into my Wernicke's area, along with the slang identified as being part of your era, daddio."

Wernicke's area. That was a part of the brain, located in the left hemisphere, that partially controlled speech and language comprehension. And she had apparently—wirelessly, no less—just injected an entire language into hers.

Wow.

"I'm, uh, impressed."

"It's nothing, dawg," she said. "I apologize for not doing so sooner. I should have been prepared for your arrival."

"You were waiting for me? How did you know—"

"Our chronal scientists were woke to the blue Doppler shift of temporal energies caused by your progress through the time stream. We've been awaiting your arrival." She held out her right hand. "I am Citizen Hefa of the Quantum Police, and it is my pleasure, Flash, to welcome you to the year 6345 for the first time."

First time? He decided to let that go and shook her hand. She seemed inordinately pleased.

"Did I do that right?" she asked a bit excitedly. "It's my first ancient ritual."

"You were fine," he told her.

She stood a little straighter, bolstered by his praise. "Thank you. I've spent my life studying deep history, so I am familiar with your primitive era, my brother. I'm afraid we have no commercially available soda water, but I took it upon myself to carbonate a distillation of vegetable extracts for your enjoyment."

She gestured, and suddenly in her hands appeared a slender glass filled with an effervescent brown liquid.

He arched an eyebrow. "You're offering me a cola?"

"My research indicates that people of your era subsisted mainly on such a concoction. Is my research not dope and fly?"

She looked so forlorn at the prospect of having gotten this detail wrong that he accepted the soda from her even though he wasn't particularly in the mood. The run from the thirtieth century *had* made him a little thirsty, though, so he took a glug of the soda. It was . . .

. . . the absolute *worst*, most disgusting thing he'd ever tasted. Like someone had soaked their sweat socks in bubbly water for a day and a half, then dumped in two cups of sugar. He managed not to gag, mindful of the hopeful, delighted expression on Hefa's face.

"I appreciate the beverage," he told her with as much earnestness as he could muster. "I'm sure your research didn't indicate this"—*because I'm making it up right now*—"but in my era, we sipped sodas in between glasses of plain water."

Her eyes widened. "Truly? You're not fronting, home-boy?"

Barry bit the inside of his cheek. It was like listening to his grandmother trying to freestyle rap. "No, I'm not, uh, fronting."

She took back the glass of cola, and it vanished, replaced by a glass of water. Barry drank the water gratefully, washing the taste of the "soda" out of his mouth, then asked, "How are you doing that?"

"Doing what?"

"Making things appear out of thin air like that."

She blinked rapidly as though he'd asked her how she was breathing or standing or something similarly obvious and idiotic. Then she relaxed. "Of course. In your time . . . I do it the same way everyone does in this time: I'm simply manipulating matter on a small scale, coercing ambient molecules into a predetermined form."

"Is everyone a metahuman in the sixty-fourth century?"

"No, no. We use quark induction. In your era, it would have been called nanotechnology."

Duh! Barry mentally slapped his forehead. Of *course!* Hocus Pocus's wand was based on a super-sophisticated, highly advanced nanotech that even Cisco hadn't been able to crack. Apparently such technology was commonplace here. Citizen Hefa didn't carry a wand, but Barry was reasonably certain that if the tech could fit into Hocus Pocus's slender little wand, there'd be no trouble embedding it in Citizen Hefa's clothes or helmet.

If everyone in the sixty-fourth century had access to such technology . . . What was this era *like?*

He stopped ruminating on the possibilities. It was pleasant to chat with Citizen Hefa of the Quantum Police, but he had a purpose in mind. He produced Hocus Pocus's wand from inside his costume and held it up. "Do people sometimes do their *quark induction* with one of these?"

At the sight of the wand, Citizen Hefa audibly groaned. It was an endearingly normal and very human thing from an era that seemed beyond normalcy and mere humanity.

"Yes," she said with a sign. "Hobicubispobicubis, formerly known as Citizen Hocu."

"He came to my era using the name 'Hocus Pocus' and caused some problems—"

"Yes. We're aware."

"I'm hoping you can help me out, then. We stopped him

and put him in a prison, but he escaped. I'm wondering if you have some way of tracking—"

He stopped speaking, for Citizen Hefa was shaking her head determinedly.

"Escaped? Oh, no. I'm terribly sorry. There's been a misunderstanding. Hobicubispobicubis did not *escape* from your prison, Flash.

"*We* let him out."

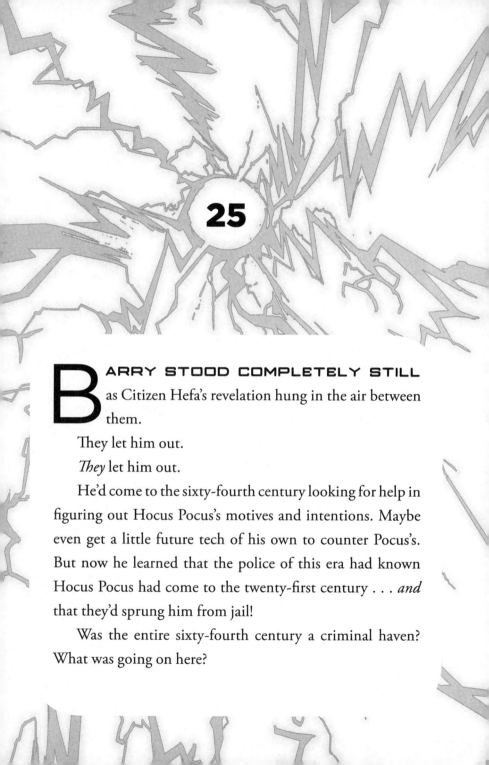

25

BARRY STOOD COMPLETELY STILL as Citizen Hefa's revelation hung in the air between them.

They let him out.

They let him out.

He'd come to the sixty-fourth century looking for help in figuring out Hocus Pocus's motives and intentions. Maybe even get a little future tech of his own to counter Pocus's. But now he learned that the police of this era had known Hocus Pocus had come to the twenty-first century . . . *and* that they'd sprung him from jail!

Was the entire sixty-fourth century a criminal haven? What was going on here?

In an instant, multiple possibilities flashed through his mind. He could escape this room, but there seemed to be no doors, and he didn't relish vibrating through one of the walls into the unknown. Or he could gamble: snatch Citizen Hefa's helmet at superspeed and hope that her nanotech was located there. Once she was powerless, he could interrogate her.

Or he could relax his internal vibrations and return instantly to the twenty-first century. But then he'd know nothing more than when he'd left home.

Last possibility: He could slow down and try talking some more.

"*You* let him out?" he demanded. "Why?"

She seemed a bit flabbergasted by his question. "Why? Because he is *our* responsibility, Flash. Our incompetence allowed him access to forbidden time transportation technology, which made it possible for him to wreak havoc in your era. I offer you and the denizens of your time period the apologies of both the Quantum Police and of the Technocracy for allowing that to happen. We are hugely chagrined for our diss." Her jaw actually trembled toward the end, and Barry thought she might break down from her rage.

"It's OK," he told her. "We handled it. For now. But why would you let him go free?"

Citizen Hefa held up both hands. One more gesture cataloged in the future: *Oh, no! You misunderstand!* "We did not let him go free, Flash. We simply teleported him through time into a secure facility of our own. Your era is not outfitted to incarcerate someone with Hobicubis-pobicubis's abilities." She paused for a moment, and some new idea lit up in her eyes. "Was the facility we plucked him from supposed to be *secure?* Then why didn't it have something as basic as shielding against sub-quarkian harmonics manipulation?"

"You got me there," Barry said.

She missed his sarcasm. Or maybe they just didn't have sarcasm anymore in the sixty-fourth century.

"Hobicubispobicubis and his ilk have caused many problems for us recently," she went on. "We Quantum Police typically regulate matter and energy. Actual crime is nearly extinct in our era, so we are ill-equipped to handle these techno-magicians and their monkeyshines."

Barry couldn't help it—a tiny giggle escaped him. "Monkeyshines?" he blurted out.

Citizen Hefa's eyes narrowed. "Isn't that the correct term from your time period? Or should I have said chicanery? Or skulduggery? Or—"

He held up a hand to stop her. It worked. Another gesture that transcended eras. "I get the point."

"True dat," she said agreeably, nearly causing him to explode with laughter.

Instead, he reminded himself to focus on the issue at hand. "You said 'and his ilk.' There are others like him?"

"Mos def, sweetie pie," Citizen Hefa said with a perfectly straight face. "Hobicubispobicubis belongs to a clan of techno-magicians, with others such as Prupesuptoupchupanupgeoup, Aliskaiszisamis, and Bisebbseidseibseobsebdseidseiseboose. They are led by the one they call their Most Exalted—"

"Abra Kadabra," Barry murmured.

"—Abhararakadhararbarakh, once known as Citizen Abra. They are all obsessed with the stage magicians of ancient history, replicating their feats and performances. But in our era, such tricks are singularly unimpressive."

That made sense. With the technology at the disposal of the average sixtieth-fourth-century citizen, magic tricks would just seem . . . banal. Who would gasp at pulling a rabbit from a hat, when *anyone* could do so with teleportation? Or stand agog at a levitation stunt when nanites meant *anyone* could defy gravity?

And suddenly, Hocus Pocus's rampage through twenty-first-century Central City made perfect sense. He had always played to the crowd. And when the crowd hadn't responded, he'd used his wand's nanotech to *make* them respond, filling his world with applause and approbation.

"So you abducted Hocus Pocus from my time and did what with him?"

Citizen Hefa opened her mouth to speak, thought better of it, paused, then said, "Why don't I show you?"

A door opened behind Barry, where there'd been no door before. He took this pretty well, he thought. He was becoming used to the future's almost blasé neglect of most laws of physics and common sense.

"After you," she said, gesturing to the door.

Barry stepped through and into a world unlike any he'd ever seen or imagined.

Only the presence of a sky—perfectly clear and shading toward nighttime—told him that he was outside. Otherwise, he would have assumed he was inside some sort of massive superstructure.

The ground beneath his feet was more like a floor: To every horizon and in every direction, it stretched out, a silvery-gray substance that yielded perfectly to each step, offering an almost sublime level of support.

At irregular intervals, spires rose from the ground, their matte surfaces stark outlines against the evening sky, colored in various pastels. Thicker at the base, tapering to needle-points, they soared to the clouds, brilliant, sharp lavenders and pinks and soft blues. They seemed to be roughly as tall as a skyscraper in his day, but some were clearly even taller, their tops vanishing into perspective and distance. Turning, he realized that he had just stepped out of one such spire, a faded red spindle maybe thirty stories high.

Citizen Hefa followed him outside. The door slid shut, its seam melding perfectly into place such that it was indistinguishable from the rest of the spire. Then, to his shock, the spire itself melted into the ground. In seconds, it was as though it had never been there.

"What *is* this place?" Barry asked her.

"I don't follow," she said, puzzled.

"I mean . . . There's nothing natural here. Just these . . . buildings, I guess? I assume we're on Earth still, but *where*?"

"Northern hemisphere, western hemisphere," she told him. "As your time period reckoned it, roughly at 44.9537° north and 93.0900° west."

That was pretty much the longitude and latitude of Central City.

He looked around again. It was like standing in the midst of an enormous Art Deco pincushion.

"I don't understand," he said. He bounced lightly on his toes to draw her attention to the strange surface on which they stood. "Without plant life, how is there any oxygen to breathe? You can't have photosynthesis, so there's no carbon cycle. And—"

Citizen Hefa touched his arm to silence him. "I'll explain," she said. "Let's walk."

She guided him off to his left. In the distance, a spire loomed tall, the trailing edge of sunlight glinting dully off its matte purple finish.

As they strolled, she explained to him that by the year 6345, the population of Earth had dwindled to a mere one billion people. Most human beings had decamped long ago for other planets or other dimensions. There was a brisk tourist trade to what she called "the hidden worlds," and Earth's surface had been lacking a large human population for a long, long time.

With all the incredible technology at their disposal, the remaining humans had turned Earth into something very close to a paradise. No one needed to work, since cheap, freely available nanotechnology provided most of life's basics. People were free to explore the arts and their own creativity, to enjoy the fruits of others', or to spend their time exploring detailed archives of the millennia of human achievement prior to the sixty-fourth century.

Barry imagined Cisco's reaction: *Yeah, how long would it take you to binge-watch thousands of years of human history?*

The spires were ad hoc structures, it turned out. Any Citizen (he could almost hear the capital *C* in her voice when she said the word) could raise one from what she called "the fecund nanopregnant substrate" for whatever purpose. Fully half the planet was covered with that "substrate," the substance on which they walked even now. It was loaded with nanites and could create almost anything needed. You could raise a spire and turn it into your house, a work space, a theater, whatever. And then collapse it back down if and when you no longer needed it. That's exactly what she'd done with the spire he had materialized into.

"Our temporal scientists knew exactly where and when you would emerge from the time stream," she told him. "I thought it might lessen your culture shock if you appeared in a room with a friendly face first."

She'd been right. He couldn't imagine his reaction if he'd stepped out of the time stream and into . . . this.

The other half of the planet, she went on, was pristinely preserved, carefully tended forest, jungle, desert, plains—the entire gamut of earthly natural habitats.

It sounded ideal. Maybe too ideal. And, sure enough, there was a serpent in this paradise.

"Abhararakadhararbarakh is the leader of the techno-wizards, the Most Exalted," Citizen Hefa told him as they continued to walk. "They've taken the idea of pursuing art to an extreme. They perform 'magic tricks' in various venues, but as I indicated earlier, the response they have been seeking has not been forthcoming.

"In our time, they've been mere pests until recently, when Hobicubispobicubis challenged Abhararakadhararbarakh for leadership of the group. They began using outlawed telepathic technology to force people to applaud their spontaneous public 'magic shows,' trying to one-up each other and see who was the best. And then Hobicubispobicubis broke into a secure government facility and used antiquated Time Cube tech from the thirtieth century to travel to your time.

"We felt this was our fault," she continued. "And so as soon as we were able to identify his unique temporal signature in deep history, we time-teleported him . . . here."

They had stopped at the spire, no longer in the distance, now right before them. Barry gazed up at its impressive height.

"And what is *here*?" he asked.

"We had to create it just for Hobicubispobicubis," she said. "Enter."

A door slid open at her command. Barry stepped inside. It was dark until Citizen Hefa joined him, at which point the lights came on.

The spire was perhaps twenty feet in diameter from the outside. On the inside, it was—impossibly—bigger, easily fifty or sixty feet across. Barry filed away the unworkable for later contemplation and just focused on what was before him.

A half wall made a smaller concentric circle within the center of the chamber. Projected out from that circle were four smallish tubes that Barry could only compare to tiny gun turrets. They pointed inward, at the center of the circle.

And there, floating in midair, lay Hocus Pocus.

Barry shuddered involuntarily at the sight of his foe, surrounded in a nimbus of pale yellow light. Pocus seemed to be sleeping peacefully, but Barry knew only too well what the man was capable of. His hand tightened around the wand.

"We had to build this spire just for him," Citizen Hefa said. "Our technology will be able to keep him from harming anyone else. Yours . . . We weren't so sure."

"It looks like he's sleeping." Citizen Hefa hadn't whispered, so Barry spoke at normal volume, even though a part of him worried it would rouse Hocus Pocus.

"In a sense. He is suspended in a light field of superdense photonic particles that have a mesmeric effect on the human brain, and he's floating in a sensory-deprivation field to eliminate stimuli."

Barry nodded thoughtfully. It seemed less barbaric than plain ol' prison or even a stint in the Pipeline. "How long will you keep him like this?"

"Until such a day comes that we can be certain he will not threaten or harm anyone. From *any* time period."

Barry heaved a sigh of relief that he hadn't even realized had coiled up within his chest. He'd been holding it in for days, ever since Hocus Pocus had vanished from the Pipeline. It had weighed him down during the entirety of his adventure on Earth 27 and then followed him into the thirtieth century and now here, where he could finally let it out, lay it down, let it go.

Some part of him had been secretly terrified of encountering Hocus Pocus again, of risking becoming the man's puppet. And now he knew for a fact that Hocus Pocus hadn't escaped, hadn't been on the loose; he'd just been transferred to a vastly superior prison, one from which he wouldn't be able to escape.

"Great," Barry said. "I thought I was gonna have to fight this guy again."

Citizen Hefa chuckled. "You'll never have to fight him again, Flash. Again, we apologize for letting him escape to your era in the first place."

"No worries," Barry said lightly. It was easy to forgive, now. "I guess I'll be headed back to—"

Of course, that's when a wall exploded.

A man in a black suit with steel-gray hair and goatee stood in the wreckage. He grinned and snapped his fingers.

"Abra Kadabra," he said, and all hell broke loose.

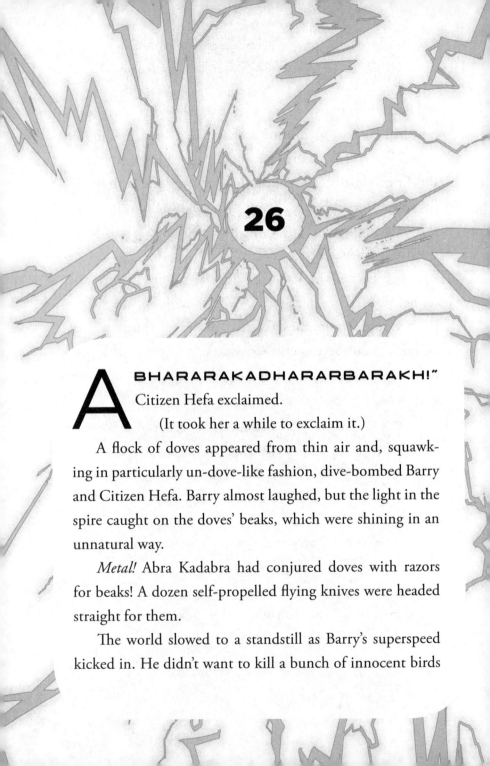

26

A BHARARAKADHARARBARAKH!" Citizen Hefa exclaimed.

(It took her a while to exclaim it.)

A flock of doves appeared from thin air and, squawking in particularly un-dove-like fashion, dive-bombed Barry and Citizen Hefa. Barry almost laughed, but the light in the spire caught on the doves' beaks, which were shining in an unnatural way.

Metal! Abra Kadabra had conjured doves with razors for beaks! A dozen self-propelled flying knives were headed straight for them.

The world slowed to a standstill as Barry's superspeed kicked in. He didn't want to kill a bunch of innocent birds that hadn't asked to be mutated and then hurled into combat, but what other option did he have?

Hmm. Yeah, he *did* have another option.

At top speed, he zipped into the cloud of doves. He grabbed two of them out of the air, careful to avoid the razor beaks. Then he raced through the hole Abra Kadabra had blown in the wall, ran halfway up the spire (it wasn't as slippery as it looked, which was a good thing), and tossed the birds into the open air.

Zoom, back down the spire, back inside. Grab two more birds. Do the whole thing again. And again. And again. Until the birds were all happily flapping and cooing somewhere in the sky above and not down in the spire where they could hurt someone.

He raced down the spire for the last time and darted back inside. By now, Kadabra had made his way to the half wall. He and Citizen Hefa were wrestling as colors swirled around them, vibrating and shimmering in the air. When Barry tried to break them up, the colors coalesced around him and smashed him against a wall.

"You can't break through a prismatic field, Flash!" Kadabra chortled. He lashed out with a fist and caught Citizen Hefa under her jaw, knocking her against the wall. She slumped down to the floor, unconscious.

"So much for the highly evolved man of the future," Barry snarled. He couldn't believe what he'd just seen. Hocus Pocus had been cruel and devious, but he'd never physically struck someone. Kadabra seemed to relish it.

"Fisticuffs are not normally to my liking," Kadabra sneered, "but needs must when a Quantum Cop can deflect your nanotech, eh? And so you've come at last to our fair century . . ." He gestured with his right hand, and a gout of fire spurted forth.

Barry dodged the flames in a split second, the tongues licking at his suit. The "prismatic field" was still swirling around Abra Kadabra, but the colors seemed dimmer. Maybe it only lasted a certain amount of time. He decided to test it; picking up a piece of debris, he chucked it at Kadabra. It exploded into dust on contact with the field, but the colors dimmed further. Yeah, it only had so much protective juice, whatever it was.

As though he didn't care, Kadabra laughed. "Tell me, Flash, did you ever figure out who Savitar was, in time to save your girlfriend's life?"

Barry had been gathering up more debris to throw, but Kadabra's comment froze him. *Savitar?* That name was familiar . . .

Right. Cisco had mentioned it. When he'd told Barry about the *other* timeline, the so-called "Flashpoint" world, where Dante was dead, Caitlin had superpowers, and the lunatic named Savitar killed people left and right.

Biting his lower lip, Barry realized he couldn't decide what to do next. A part of him wanted to stop and think about this—if Kadabra knew about Savitar, then had he slipped into a different timeline, after all?—but the greater part of him knew that he had to stop Kadabra.

Who was in whose timeline? Or were they both in someone else's? Did it even really matter?

"Well, Flash?" Kadabra asked, leering. "Were you able to save your lady love from Savitar's clutches? History is divided on this point, so I'd love to hear it from you personally how you felt when you finally pulled off Savitar's mask and saw the face of evil."

"I think you have me confused with another Barry Allen," Barry said. "But I imagine that guy would be OK with me doing this."

Rapid-fire, he threw one-two-three-four pieces of debris at Kadabra, watching the prismatic field weaken with each hit. As soon as the fifth piece of debris left his hand, he was on a tear, racing the jagged chunk of metal toward Abra Kadabra.

He kept pace with it but let the debris hit first. The prismatic field dimmed further, almost transparent now. Too late, Abra Kadabra realized what the Flash had done, just as Barry threw his hands up to protect his face and crashed through the last remnants of the prismatic field. It felt like diving into a pool filled with salt and razor blades, but he was through, and he enjoyed the moment of terror on Kadabra's face as he swung his fist, landing a devastating blow on the magician's jaw.

Or at least, he *thought* it was devastating. His passage through the prismatic field had slowed him down more than he realized. Abra Kadabra staggered backward and fetched up against the half wall, but he wasn't knocked out, just knocked off-kilter. Barry lunged at him again, but his fist went through nothing but air and an echoing, mocking laugh.

Spinning around, he saw Kadabra behind him. At a snap of the magician's fingers, a high-powered jet of water came from nowhere and knocked Barry off his feet, sending him careening into the half wall, then spilling over it and into the containment area. He caught his breath, ducked under the forceful blast of water, then threw himself forward, phasing his way through the half wall.

On the other side, there were ten Abra Kadabras waiting for him.

I hate *holograms!* Barry thought.

He spun his arms and directed the whirlwinds that resulted at the Kadabras. Three of them were the closest, and none of them so much as had a hair budge out of place when the wind hit them. Fakes.

He moved to his left, still spinning, still throwing out wind. Two more didn't move. Half of them down. The real Kadabra was among the last five.

There was no need to blast those five—one of them broke away from the others, gesturing wildly. Barry looked up and beheld flaming meteors dropping down from the ceiling.

You're kidding me.

He could vibrate to let them pass through him, but Citizen Hefa wasn't so lucky. So he ran a circuit of the room, picking up speed as he did so, funneling air down and away from the flaming rocks Abra Kadabra had conjured. Lacking oxygen, they extinguished before they hit the floor. Barry gracefully dodged one of them and punched another with a vibrating hand, shattering it into a million harmless pieces before it could crush Citizen Hefa.

There was suddenly a slight popping sound nearby. Before Barry could react, Abra Kadabra—standing right next to him—reached out and snatched Hocus Pocus's wand.

"I'll take that." With another nearly inaudible *pop!*, the magician vanished.

Barry whirled around, seeking Kadabra, and now found him standing on the other side of the half wall, near Hocus Pocus.

"That the best you've got?" Barry taunted. Mocking villains sometimes tripped them up and made them make dumb mistakes.

Kadabra chortled. "Hardly. But it's all I need."

With that, he raised his arms and snapped the fingers on both hands at once. In less than the blink of a Flash's eye, both Kadabra and Pocus vanished.

Barry sighed and shook his head. "Yeah," he said to the unconscious Quantum Police officer at his feet. "I *knew* he was gonna do that."

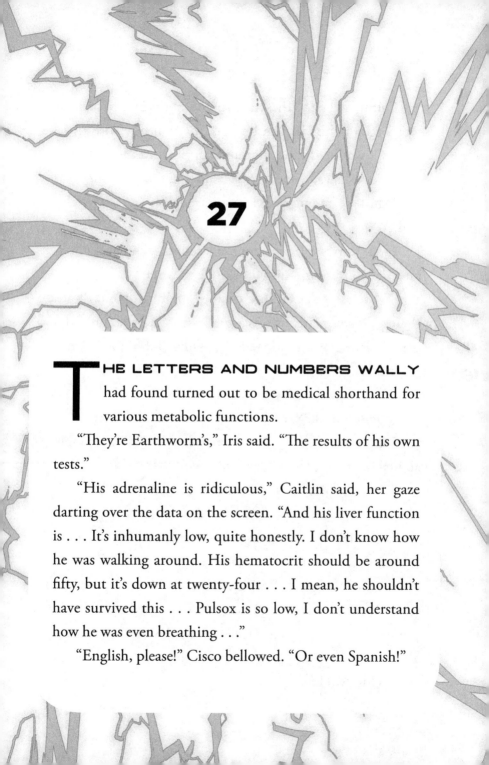

27

THE LETTERS AND NUMBERS WALLY
had found turned out to be medical shorthand for
various metabolic functions.

"They're Earthworm's," Iris said. "The results of his own
tests."

"His adrenaline is ridiculous," Caitlin said, her gaze
darting over the data on the screen. "And his liver function
is . . . It's inhumanly low, quite honestly. I don't know how
he was walking around. His hematocrit should be around
fifty, but it's down at twenty-four . . . I mean, he shouldn't
have survived this . . . Pulsox is so low, I don't understand
how he was even breathing . . ."

"English, please!" Cisco bellowed. "Or even Spanish!"

Caitlin sighed. "These are the numbers of a patient in total organ failure. If you brought me someone with these results, I would assume shutdown or near-shutdown of the liver and kidneys, with the heart and lungs next on the list."

"Must be tough to get around without those," Wally said.

"You saw the guy jumping around, though," Cisco mused. "He sure was spry for a dude without—"

"We're idiots!" Caitlin exclaimed, bolting up out of her chair. "Of *course* his organs were in a state of failure. The particle accelerator irradiated him, killing off his body from the inside out."

"But he's still walking around . . ." Wally said.

"Right. Think. What's he been doing to his victims?"

Iris got there first. "Wait. You mean, he's killing people and taking their organs . . . for himself?"

"How the heck do you do *that?*" Cisco demanded. "He's gotta have a friend, right? Another doctor who can put him under and transplant the organs. He can't possibly be doing it himself . . . can he?"

Caitlin shrugged. "When death is knocking at the front door, and there's no back door, you make a window pretty quick. He's dying. He's *been* dying since the accelerator explosion. Everything he's done since then has been to extend his own life."

The room fell silent. H.R., mid-hustle to Iris's side with a large steaming mug, said, "Makes you feel sorry for him."

"Maybe," Iris put in, accepting the coffee. "If he weren't killing people to survive."

"There is that," H.R. agreed.

Cisco pounded at his keyboard and brought up a scrolling list of all the Earthworm victims they'd identified to date. "Now, Dr. Snow, I'm not a medical doctor, but I believe the human body only contains *two* kidneys, correct?"

"Last time I counted," she said.

"Well, our friend Herbie has taken a total of *five* kidneys over the past few years. Is he making a pie?"

"Gross!" Wally and Iris said at the same time.

"Oh, no, not at all," H.R. said. "A nice steak and kidney pie is a delight, especially if the mushrooms are fresh and you sauté the kidney just right, and, oh, wait, you're talking about *human* kidneys. Never mind; I was never here." He slinked out of the Cortex.

"Five kidneys," Caitlin mused. She planted her hands on her hips and stared up at the screen. "And *two* livers."

"And four stomachs," Wally added.

"Three gallbladders," Iris put in. "Only one of those per person, if I remember high school biology correctly."

"You do," Caitlin assured her. "Which means . . ." She went pale, swallowing hard. "He's doing multiple transplants. Whatever the accelerator did to him, it's still happening; it's ongoing."

"Let me get this straight," Cisco said slowly. "Doc Hynde gets hit by the dark-matter wave, which apparently increases his speed, strength, and agility *and* gives him the bizarre but useful ability to talk to rats. At the same time, it not only parboils his organs, but also causes any *new* organs to rot, as well?"

"This guy picked the worst numbers you can imagine in the metahuman lottery," Iris said.

"True dat," Cisco agreed.

Wally groaned. "I thought we talked about *true dat*."

"Is that on the list of things I'm not supposed to say?"

"You sound like an idiot when you say it."

"True *dat*?" Cisco tried. "*True* dat?"

"Just give it up." Wally waved him off.

Caitlin ignored them and returned to her computer. Scanning the documents, she mentally kicked herself.

"These are all statistics and data on organ matching. He was using his laptop to hack into the CCGH patient database and track people who were potential donors for him."

"Is *donor* the right word for something involuntary?" Iris asked.

"Probably not," Caitlin conceded. "He's got a kidney list, for example, where he's matching tissue types for common

HLA antigens, looking for negative lymphocytotoxic cross-match . . ." She shook her head. "They're all like this. For every organ. Searching for CMV and EBV negativity for intestinal matches . . . He's got his own information in, and he runs pattern matching on the right medical parameters against CCGH's database."

Cisco shivered. "He's programmed evil. Turned it into an algorithm. How efficient."

"The personal journey entries deteriorate as time goes by," Wally put in. "I mean, I'm looking at one from, like, six months after the particle accelerator explosion. Check it."

He sent the entry to the big screen. It read:

true self now open and real and true and real
sunlight is overrated shades pulled stay here in dark
belong in the Downworld
Upworld is for prey I am no prey
I am predator
so go
go down
go down for hunt
dark dark hunt

"Earthworms aren't predators," Cisco mused. "Why would someone who thinks of himself as a predator call himself *Earthworm*?"

"Maybe he doesn't." It was Iris, chiming in from her seat. "One of his victims scratched that word into the sewer wall that Wally found. *They* called him Earthworm."

"Maybe because he regenerates?" Cisco wondered. "If you cut an earthworm in half, two of them will grow from the halves. Maybe that's why."

"That's not even true," Wally scoffed. "It's an old wives' tale."

"Is not!"

"Is so."

Cisco's fingers danced on his keyboard. "We'll check that authoritative voice, my close personal friend, the Internet, and . . . Oh. Oh." He cleared his throat. "Never mind. We don't have time for this nonsense."

Wally cracked a grin. "Told you."

"Guys, it doesn't matter *why* he's Earthworm," Caitlin reminded them. "What matters is where he is and how we stop him."

That summoned a pall of silence over the Cortex. They'd been hunting Earthworm for close to a week, and other than knowing that he was in the sewers somewhere, they had nothing. Wally had found him at one location, true, but surely Earthworm wouldn't return to that spot, now that it had been compromised.

Whether intentionally or by accident, their foe had chosen the best possible place to hide. The metal pipes and heavy concrete of the sewers made electronic surveillance and reconnaissance difficult, if not impossible. And superspeed was useless down there. Too many turns and twists, jagged little corridors, webs of hefty piping, narrow sluice gates, and more. An ideal spot for Earthworm.

"What we need," Iris said at last, "is a way to think like him."

No one spoke for a moment. Cisco tugged at his unfamiliar ponytail absentmindedly. "You intrigue me, Ms. West. Go on."

Iris pursed her lips, thinking. "I mean . . . He's got to have a base of operations down there, right? He only comes up to use his computer when he needs to because he doesn't want to be aboveground. Like the journal entry Wally found says. He belongs to the 'Downworld.'"

"But he has to have somewhere that he calls home," Caitlin agreed. "Or lair. Or whatever. A permanent base of operations. Somewhere to sleep, if nothing else. To eat. He has to do those things; he's still human. Marginally," she hastened to add before anyone could disagree.

"We used the data about his latest victims to figure out where he's been recently," Wally said. "And it worked. I found him there. Is there a way to use the same data to figure out where he is *usually*?"

Wally, Iris, and Caitlin turned to look at Cisco. H.R. chose that moment to reenter the Cortex. "Are we staring at Cisco?" he asked. "OK." He leaned against the wall and fixed his most penetrating gaze on Cisco . . .

. . . who held his hands up in mock surrender. "Guys! I'm flattered that you think so highly of me, but we need a *lot* more data than that. There are miles and miles of sewer down there."

"We *have* more data," Caitlin said emphatically, gesturing to her screen. "We know now that he's using CCGH's database to match patients to his own transplant needs. So that means we can search records back to the accelerator explosion and find any organ-removal cases where the victim is within Herbie's tolerance for transplant."

Cisco nodded. "Yeah, that's better than just a list of *all* victims. But it's still not enough."

Wally whooped with joy and slapped his hand on the desk. "What about if we know the exact day he went into the sewers?" he asked, eyes shining. "I've got a journal entry here: 'Downworld now Downworld always forever Upworld no more darkness takes me and I take it.' It's time-stamped and everything."

Cisco clucked his tongue and rocked back and forth, back and forth. "So," he said slowly, "we theoretically know exactly who his victims are, where and when he grabbed them, where and when he dumped the bodies. Which gives us some locations to work with. And if we know *when* he started living in the sewers . . ." He trailed off, his eyes going blank and staring as they often did when he was building something in his mind.

The stare went on for a long time. Wally started tapping his foot slightly, then faster; then it became a blur. Iris elbowed him and told him to knock it off.

"Cisco?" Caitlin said. "Earth to Cisco . . ."

"It's not as easy as it sounds," Cisco said.

"I didn't think it sounded easy at all," H.R. said to a chorus of agreements.

Cisco spun around in his chair and began playing the keyboard like a virtuoso. "Have to take into account storm surges," he said. "'Cause that could change where he decided to hang his hat when he moved to Casa del Stinky. So, gotta grab weather data. Also need maintenance work schedules from the city's department of public works database. So, yeah, hack that. And don't forget to consider—"

"Cisco!" Iris barked. "Are you saying you can do it?"

Cisco smirked with the old Ramon confidence. "When have I ever *not* been able to do it?"

167

Iris looked at her watch. It was almost midnight. Twelve hours to the CCPD disciplinary hearing, and still no Barry.

Stop worrying about his job, Iris. Start worrying about his life.

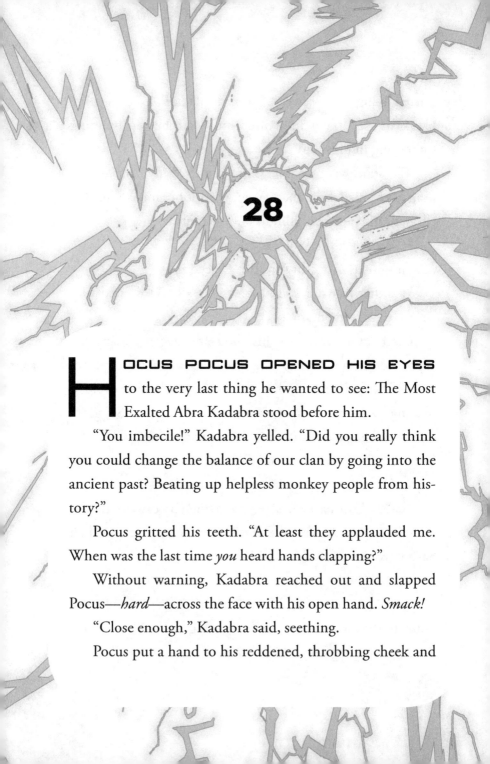

28

HOCUS POCUS OPENED HIS EYES to the very last thing he wanted to see: The Most Exalted Abra Kadabra stood before him.

"You imbecile!" Kadabra yelled. "Did you really think you could change the balance of our clan by going into the ancient past? Beating up helpless monkey people from history?"

Pocus gritted his teeth. "At least they applauded me. When was the last time *you* heard hands clapping?"

Without warning, Kadabra reached out and slapped Pocus—*hard*—across the face with his open hand. *Smack!*

"Close enough," Kadabra said, seething.

Pocus put a hand to his reddened, throbbing cheek and

ground his teeth. "That is the last time I'll let you touch me without consequence." He balled his hands into fists.

"I just rescued you from the Quantum Cops' sleep-forever version of prison. Gratitude is in order, I believe." Kadabra took a step back from Pocus. "But don't mistake my brotherly concern for one of our own for actual affection, Hocus Pocus. No one is indispensable. I'll happily return you to the tender mercies of the Quantum Police, if you prefer."

Gnashing his teeth and leaning in toward Kadabra, Pocus shouted, "You'll do *nothing*! *I* am Abra Kadabra now! *I* traveled in time! *I* defeated the Flash and saw him grovel before me!"

Kadabra raised an eyebrow. "Oh? Then tell me, 'Most Exalted Hocus Pocus,' why is the Flash here?"

Pocus took a step back, hands now slack at his sides. "What did you say?"

"The Flash," Kadabra said with sinister glee. "Here. In the sixty-fourth century. With a Quantum Cop, in *your* prison spire. If you crushed him so egregiously, what is he doing here?"

"I defeated him," Pocus said, weakly. "I suffered a set-back, yes, but—"

"You defeated yourself and no one else!" Kadabra said,

his lips twisted into a disgusted sneer. "You don't deserve this!" He waved Pocus's wand in his face.

And Pocus grabbed it.

He enjoyed Abra Kadabra's startled expression as he plucked the wand right out of his hand. With no time to spare, he waved the wand and teleported behind Kadabra.

"As they say in the Flash's era," Pocus said when Kadabra spun around, "would you like to take this outside?"

29

THEY SLEPT AT S.T.A.R. LABS, SACKING out on beds in the medical bay or cots in the workshops. Everyone wanted to be available as soon as Cisco's program finished running.

To their surprise, they got a full eight hours of sleep, crashing at two in the morning when Cisco finished writing the program and sent it off into the digital ether to do its work. Joe woke them all when he arrived at ten, done with his late shift, bearing a sack of bagels and a big take-out box of coffee from C.C. Jitters.

"Bless you, Joseph West!" H.R. grabbed the coffee, held it over his upturned, open mouth, and went to twist open the tap.

Joe snatched it away from him. "That's for everyone, H.R."

"H.R. needing his precioussss," H.R. rasped in his

best Gollum imitation, which earned him a rare approving thumbs-up from Cisco.

As H.R. and Joe battled over the disposition of the coffee, Iris glared around the room. "I thought you set an alarm that would wake us up when the program finished running," she grumped.

"Someone got up on the wrong side of the orthopedic hospital bed," Cisco said. "And the alarm didn't go off because the program's still running." He made a *voila!* motion at the big screen, which showed the words SYSTEM PROCESSING in flashing red letters.

"It's been hours!" Iris complained.

"There's a lot of data to crunch," Cisco said defensively. "A lot of fuzzy logic. I had to code a dedicated neural net and adapt a system of machine learning—"

"Stop it!" Iris slammed her palm down on a desk. Everyone jumped. Off in a corner, H.R. and Joe went still.

"Iris . . ." Caitlin approached her. "We're all jittery and on edge, but . . ."

Iris pulled away from Caitlin, shoulders hunched in defeat. In her hand, she held Barry's cell phone, which she stared at as though it had the answers to all Life's questions.

"Nothing is happening," she said. "Nothing at all."

"The program will finish," Cisco said gently. "And when it does, we'll be able to move on Earthworm."

"Quickly," Wally put in. "*Super* quickly."

Iris shook her head. "No. Not enough. I can't take this anymore. The waiting. I have to do something," she whispered. "We can't catch Earthworm. We can't save Barry. I have to do *something*." A moment passed, and then she stood upright, straightened her clothes, and headed for the corridor that led to the exit elevator.

"Where are you going?" Joe shouted after her.

"I'm going to Barry's hearing," she called back. "Maybe *he* can't be there to plead on his behalf, but someone should."

Joe stood at the doorway, pulled in both directions. His responsibility as a cop told him to wait for Cisco's program to finish. His onus as a father ordered him to follow Iris.

Finally, he set the coffee down on the floor, shrugged, and looked back into the Cortex helplessly. "Guys . . ."

The Cortex went silent. Cisco and Wally exchanged a look. Caitlin turned to H.R., who had actually turned away from the promise of coffee to gaze on his friends with a resolute expression.

"I'll fire up my face-changing gizmo," H.R. said firmly, "'cause I'm going with you." No one said another word. No one needed to. With one thought shared among them, they all followed Joe out into the corridor, trailing Iris as she made for the elevator.

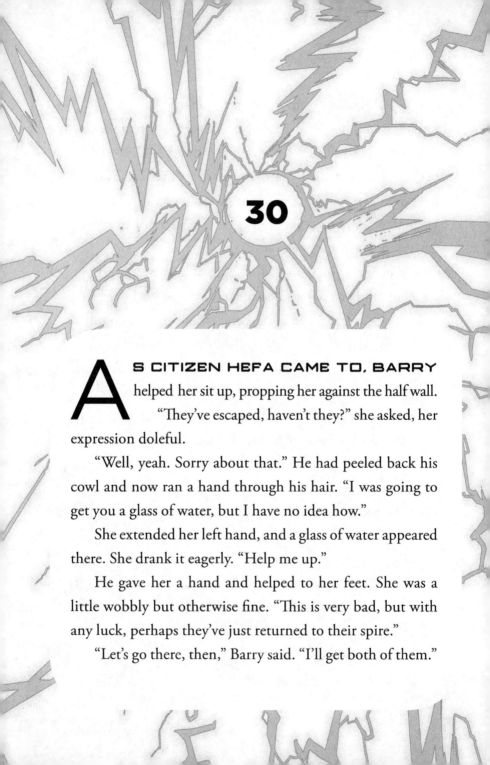

30

AS CITIZEN HEFA CAME TO, BARRY helped her sit up, propping her against the half wall.

"They've escaped, haven't they?" she asked, her expression doleful.

"Well, yeah. Sorry about that." He had peeled back his cowl and now ran a hand through his hair. "I was going to get you a glass of water, but I have no idea how."

She extended her left hand, and a glass of water appeared there. She drank it eagerly. "Help me up."

He gave her a hand and helped to her feet. She was a little wobbly but otherwise fine. "This is very bad, but with any luck, perhaps they've just returned to their spire."

"Let's go there, then," Barry said. "I'll get both of them."

"There's no point. The entrance is encrypted. We can't get in."

"I can. I can vibrate through."

"No." She shook her head, then thought better of it, still woozy from being knocked out. "You don't understand. You may have noticed that the spires are bigger on the inside than on the outside."

"You mean they *look* bigger." Yes, as he'd entered the prison, he'd thought it seemed larger on the inside, all right, but that was impossible.

"No, I mean they *are* bigger." She gestured around them. "Spires are identical on the outside, but the insides are custom crafted for or by individuals and are actually located in a subdimension. Each spire forms its own under-space, adjacent to our own. It's a portal, not a building. So if you try to vibrate through the wall, you'll just end up scattered through the many subdimensions of under-space."

Barry turned around to point, meaning to show her how Kadabra had managed to come through the wall, but he realized even as he did so that Kadabra had dramatically blown through the *door*.

"With Hobicubispobicubis free," Citizen Hefa went on, "the clan of techno-magicians is complete again. Who knows what sort of havoc they'll wreak."

"It might not be that bad," Barry said. "In my time, it seemed like Hocus Pocus wanted to *supplant* Abra Kadabra. He even started calling himself Abra Kadabra, toward the end."

Citizen Hefa reacted to this with a blank stare. "He . . . he did *what?*"

"I'm just saying," Barry went on, "that maybe they'll just be bickering among themselves and—"

"This is *terrible!*" Citizen Hefa said. "It will be a war of the techno-magicians!"

Outside, the sky was on fire.

It had gone red and yellow and orange, as though the sun had somehow decided to re-rise. Maybe that was possible in the far-flung future, but Barry doubted it.

No, he was pretty sure the sky was on fire because of the two figures floating a hundred feet straight up—one in white, the other in black—lobbing lightning bolts and fireballs at each other.

Hocus Pocus and Abra Kadabra.

Barry groaned. One of them had been enough of a headache. Now he had *two* of them to deal with!

"I don't get it," Barry said. "They're fighting like this over who gets to be called *Abra Kadabra?* What's all the fuss?"

"You would not understand," Citizen Hefa said. "In this

time period, names are of utmost importance. Names connect to status, privilege, possessions . . . Hobicubispobicubis has always envied Abhararakadhararbarakh's status in society, as well as among other techno-wizards. If he can assume Abhararakadhararbarakh's name, then he will take on Abhararakadhararbarakh's power and prestige, as well. He will become the sum of both of them, more powerful and more dangerous than either of them could be separately. He will assume control of the Magicians'—"

She broke off as lightning cracked overhead. "We have to clear this area!" Citizen Hefa said.

Barry looked around. Other than the two combatants, he and Citizen Hefa were the only people there. "I don't follow you."

Citizen Hefa pointed to one spire after another. "There are people inside each of those spires. If the techno-magicians do enough damage to a structure, it'll lose its connection to its unique subdimension, and there's a good chance the people inside will never be able to get back."

Barry hopped up and down on his toes. Above, Hocus Pocus had just launched an enormous wave of water at Abra Kadabra. As a result, it started to rain about twenty yards away. Barry figured this was probably the only rain this part of the world had seen in decades, maybe centuries.

"What do we do, then? I can go door-to-door—"

"There are only doors when someone who raised a spire or is authorized wants one," Citizen Hefa told him. "I need to do something unprecedented." She took a deep breath and balled up her fists. Barry braced himself and dug in his heels, ready to take off and offer whatever assistance he could.

"Hello, Citizens," said Citizen Hefa very, very calmly, "this is the Quantum Police with an emergency alert. This is neither a drill nor a test. Everyone within the range of this broadcast, please exit your spires and move to safe territory at coordinates thirteen-alpha-twenty. Thank you for your cooperation."

Barry stared at her.

Her lips downturned in a melancholy frown, she looked down at her feet. "I can't believe I had to do that," she mumbled.

"What are you *talking* about?" Barry demanded. He flung a hand out at the range of spires around them. "We have to *do* something! People need to—"

He broke off. All around him, doors opened in the sides of spires, and people spilled out. Where before there had been only Citizen Hefa and he (and, of course, what Cisco would no doubt have already dubbed *The Magical Flying Menaces*), there were now dozens—no, wait, *hundreds*—of people clustered on the weird, flat, spire-pocked plain that made up what had once been Central City.

This he could deal with. He didn't know what "coordinates thirteen-alpha-twenty" meant, but moving people from a danger zone to a safe zone was Flash Action 101. It was basic, first-day stuff, and, sure, there were a lot of people, but he'd done this many, many times. He knew what to do.

At top speed, he bolted for the rapidly growing crowd of sixty-fourth-century Citizens, reaching out to grab the first one and haul her off to safety. Just as his fingers brushed against her arm, though, he felt a tingling sensation go up to his elbow. Before his eyes, the woman he'd been so intent on saving vanished, blinking out of his existence at a speed that caught even the Flash off guard.

Well, OK.

He'd already picked his second rescue target. With speed like his, it always paid to plan ahead in order to maximize efficiency, so in big-crowd rescue scenarios, he pre-plotted the initial ten or so rescues so that he wouldn't waste precious micro-seconds figuring out whom to snatch up next in those first crucial moments. He juked slightly to his left and put his hand on a man's shoulder . . .

Only to get the tingling again. The man disappeared.

Barry spun around. All around him, in every direction, Citizens were melting into the air, slipping away before he could get to them.

Teleporting. Of course. Rescuing themselves faster than he could rescue them.

It was gratifying to see it but also a little frustrating. What was *he* supposed to do?

Just then, he heard a bellow from above, and a frozen ball of *something* hurtled from the sky, peeling off flecks of ice and steam so frigid, it could burn. One of the wizards had conjured what looked to be the core of a comet.

They're creative; I'll give them that much.

Barry scoped out the situation quickly. Most of the crowd was gone. The comet head would hit with great impact but no harm to anyone. In the meantime, he knew without a doubt what he needed to do. He needed to get up into the sky and stop this battle before it spilled into farther territory and risked more lives.

Twenty-first century or sixty-fourth, the job was the same.

He ran up the nearest spire. With powers like his, science was crucial, and math was a necessity, especially trigonometry. You had to figure out the angles, the best ways to use your considerable momentum to get to places flat-out speed couldn't manage. As fast as Barry could move, he couldn't fly, so he relied on being able to calculate angles in his head, a trick that had moderately impressed his teachers in middle school but was now a literal lifesaver.

It was basically like turning your body into a billiard ball that could break the sound barrier, and the world was a weirdly shaped pool table.

Halfway up the spire, he pushed off, twisting in the air like a high-diver, then somersaulting at the last moment. His feet came down on the comet. He felt the burn of the cold for just an instant as he pushed off with all his strength, flinging himself through the empty air. He had just enough juice left for another flip, landing with his feet on the vertical surface of another spire. Before gravity could blink and say, "Hey, wait a second!" Barry raced farther up the side of the spire, ran partway around its circumference, and jumped again, aiming at a new spire.

In this manner, he ping-ponged himself back and forth from spire to spire along his pre-calculated route, dashing up sides just long enough to build up the right amount of momentum to let him launch himself at the next spire. Until, finally, his target wasn't a spire anymore.

Nope, not a spire at all.

With plenty of force at his back, he shoved off from the tip of the last spire. With his arms held straight at his sides, he was like a red-clad humanoid missile flying through the air on a perfect arc that carried him right to his target.

At the last possible second, he tucked into a ball, lowered his head, and twisted his shoulder forward. Right on schedule, he slammed into Abra Kadabra.

Bodychecking Kadabra wasn't nearly as satisfying as doing the same to Hocus Pocus would have been, but he would take what he could get. This was where the angles and momentum and possibilities took him. Boom. Right into Kadabra's back.

The magician gasped and flailed and staggered in the sky. Then he began to plummet, dropping like a stone.

Of course, Barry did the same. Fast was fast, but eventually gravity caught up. Gravity *always* caught up.

But sometimes you could keep fooling it, for just a little while, at least. If he'd calculated correctly . . .

He dropped for a split second, then brought his feet down on Kadabra's back as the magician fell. With a mighty heave, he launched himself back up into the air and just barely managed to snag one of Hocus Pocus's feet.

"Get off of me!" Pocus howled, thrashing his feet in rage.

"Nah," Barry said and he held on tighter, now using both hands.

Whatever nano-wizardry Pocus was using to stay afloat, it was clearly designed to hold up *his* weight and not much else. With gratifying speed, the two of them started drifting down to the ground. Barry risked a quick peek down. He was up higher than he'd realized, and vertigo made his head swim for a moment, but then he shook it off and was pleased to see a tiny dot on the ground below. Abra Kadabra was already down for the count.

"This time I won't just defeat you," Hocus Pocus raged. "This time I'll *destroy* you!" He waved his wand, and a blast of energy exploded forth.

Barry managed to swing off to one side, still gripping Pocus's calf. The energy beam sizzled by him, singeing the left arm of his suit but otherwise doing no harm.

"Brush up on your ancient history, Pocus! You didn't defeat anyone. We beat you."

"You *cheated*! You had help!" Pocus wound up his wand-arm again, a devilish gleam in his eye. Even as they picked up speed in their free fall, all he could think about was hurting Barry.

"Your one-track mind is gonna get you killed one of these days," Barry warned him. He pulled with all his strength and managed to "climb" up Pocus's body a bit, just far enough to get a hand around the magician's wrist and tilt the wand so that the beam of *whatever* he'd been ready to fire at Barry instead shot off harmlessly into the air.

"Maybe try killing me less and not hitting the ground more," Barry suggested. The ground was rising up at them at a concerning, brisk pace.

As if he'd just realized they were falling, Pocus cursed, gestured again, and blinked away as though plucked out of the sky by an invisible giant, leaving Barry falling on his own.

Terrific.

Abra Kadabra still lay there on the ground below him.

Barry started churning his legs as fast as he could, whipping up a cushion of air beneath him. It slowed him down just enough that when he hit the ground, it only felt like falling from a second-story window, not from over a hundred stories straight up. Still, it knocked the breath out of him for a moment.

When he managed to collect himself enough to stand, he saw only Citizen Hefa. "Where did Kadabra go?"

"Teleported away as soon as he regained consciousness," she said, coming over to him.

"Do you have backup coming?"

It took her a moment to figure out what he meant. Clearly the idea of *backup* wasn't a typical conversation topic. "There are other Quantum Police officers coming from other sectors, yes. But personal teleportation is a short-range technology. They are hep to the danger, but it will take them several jumps to get here."

Barry sighed in resignation. He stretched, feeling his ribs ache. "All right, then. What do we do in the meantime? If teleportation is a short-range tech, where did the magicians go? They have to be nearby, right?"

"Within thirty kilometers or so, yes," Citizen Hefa explained. "No doubt they've returned to their spire to lick their wounds. But their battle will once again spill out into the world, endangering innocent Citizens." She stood quietly for a moment. "There is no need for you to remain, Flash. You've done more than you should have. Return to your time period. Live your life. Let me and my fellow officers handle this."

"Not a chance." He didn't even have to take the time to think about it. "Doing my job can be tough, but at its core, the job itself is conceptually really, really simple. Are there people in danger? If yes, then I get to work. I don't make a distinction between people in different cities or different countries or even different universes. I can't see any reason I should do so just because I'm in the future."

Citizen Hefa considered him for a moment, then nodded once. "Thank you, Flash. You are as woke and fab and gear as the legends portray."

"Glad to live up to the history books," Barry told her. "Show me the magicians' spire."

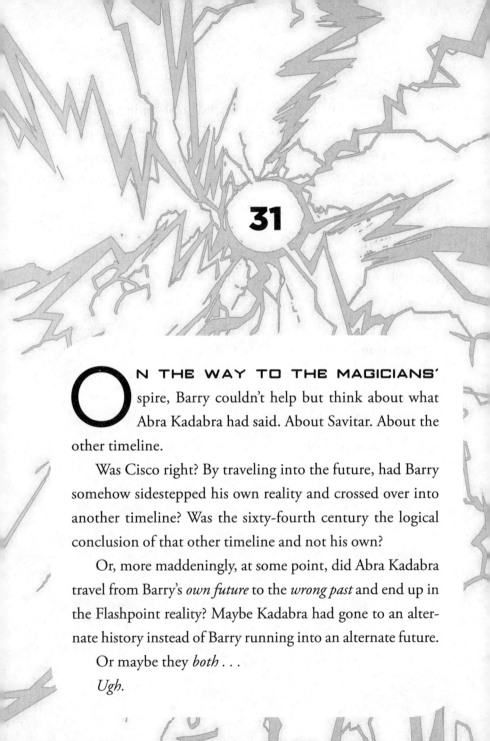

31

ON THE WAY TO THE MAGICIANS' spire, Barry couldn't help but think about what Abra Kadabra had said. About Savitar. About the other timeline.

Was Cisco right? By traveling into the future, had Barry somehow sidestepped his own reality and crossed over into another timeline? Was the sixty-fourth century the logical conclusion of that other timeline and not his own?

Or, more maddeningly, at some point, did Abra Kadabra travel from Barry's *own future* to the *wrong past* and end up in the Flashpoint reality? Maybe Kadabra had gone to an alternate history instead of Barry running into an alternate future.

Or maybe they *both* . . .

Ugh.

It went beyond migraine territory and straight to set-your-brain-on-fire. There were infinite possibilities and no way to determine which was real. He shoved those thoughts away, determined to return to them when he had less on his plate.

The magicians' spire hovered into view before him. It was nothing like what Barry expected. He'd thought it would be a smallish, low-key affair, most likely executed in black or maybe just muted gray tones. Something designed not to attract attention, a building made to conceal its nature and the nature of those within. Your basic criminal hideout, in other words.

But . . . not so much.

The magicians' spire was the tallest within sight, rising to a needle point that seemed to poke right through the sky. It gleamed with a kaleidoscope of colors and patterns—bright blues, resplendent yellows, fervent reds, glowing greens. Drifting around it in a perpetual loop, a series of holograms spelled out something that Citizen Hefa translated as, "WORLDS OF ENCHANTMENT AND BEWONDERMENT WITHIN!"

Unlike every other spire he'd seen, this one had a very large, very obvious, very bright orange *door*.

Of course. These guys wanted attention. They wanted an audience and applause.

But they weren't idiots. The door was securely locked.

"So, can we force the door somehow?" Barry asked. Surely the Quantum Police had some sort of security override that would allow them entrance to the spire.

"Force the door?" Citizen Hefa's perplexed expression told him everything he needed to know. Those words just didn't combine into anything sensible. Even the very idea of barging in there was foreign to her.

"You have no way of breaking in?" he asked. "Really?" He thought of the cops in his own time, with their battering rams and carefully placed explosive charges that could knock doors off their hinges. Ugly displays of primitive brute force, yes. But they worked.

"Breaking in?" she said in the same tone she'd used to say *Force the door?* Thanks to her download of English, they could understand each other's words, but apparently some concepts just didn't jibe here in the sixty-fourth century.

"In my time, the police can—if they have to—use, uh, whatever means necessary in order to get into a criminal's home or hideout," Barry told her. "You Quantum Police have no such capabilities?"

Citizen Hefa looked slightly ill at the very notion. "The privacy of Citizens is paramount in our time, Flash. I understand that in your era, individual liberties were restricted, but in our time, this isn't the case."

It didn't make any sense to argue with her further. In

an era in which any Citizen could "raise a spire" and use nanotechnology to accouter it in any fashion, yeah, crime was probably at an all-time low, with police powers being lowered accordingly. No point fighting over it.

But, there was something . . . Something she'd said that jogged his memory . . .

Ah, yes! "When I first came here, you told me that Hocus Pocus was *formerly* known as Citizen Hocu. So am I right that his various . . . misbehaviors have caused his citizenship to be revoked?"

"Yes." Citizen Hefa bobbed her head. "Many of the techno-magicians have had their citizenships terminated."

"What, exactly, does that mean?"

"Their spires are decommissioned, locked into their current shapes and configurations. But they still have the right to remain within."

Barry groaned and kicked at the synthetic ground. "Come on!" he complained. "You mean there's nothing we can do to stop these guys?"

Citizen Hefa pulled herself up to her full height and locked eyes with him. "Flash, I understand that in your era, there were . . . expediencies. But our time prioritizes liberty and freedom from the state."

Barry ran a hand through his hair. It was a different time. A *way* different time. So much advanced technology . . . so few people on the planet . . . Of course attitudes about law and order would be different. And of course the legal needs of the people would change.

"I'm sorry I lost my temper," he said. "It's just frustrating. I don't want these guys to be able to cause any further hassles for you and for your people."

She nodded in agreement. "Our age is idealistic. Maybe even naive, considering. We are not equipped to handle—" She broke off as a figure blinked into existence a few yards from the door to the magicians' spire. It was a man, short and squat, wearing a tuxedo that would have been considered outdated even in Barry's time, as well as a threadbare top hat. As Barry and Citizen Hefa watched, the portly fellow waddled to the door.

"Who's that?"

"Aliskaiszisamis," Citizen Hefa said. "Citizen Ali. He still possesses his citizenship. We can't arrest him."

Barry's palms itched. He wanted to arrest *someone*.

As he watched, Aliskaiszisamis stood before the door. The techno-magician paused, then turned to wave cheerily at Barry and Citizen Hefa. Barry resisted the urge to super-speed to the man's side and shake him until some useful intel fell out.

Citizen Ali rummaged in the pockets of his tuxedo for a moment, then produced something small and flat.

He held it out at arm's length, and the door to the spire opened.

"Wait, what did he just do?" Barry asked. Citizen Hefa had opened doors with what appeared to be mere gestures. Citizen Ali had had something like a remote control.

"Token access," Citizen Hefa said. "The Citizen who raises a spire controls entrance to it, but there are automatic systems that can be engaged to recognize passphrases, faces, and so on. The techno-magicians use such a system for their spire."

Barry licked his lips. "Then if we can find out what they use to get in . . ." He trailed off to let Citizen Hefa get the idea.

It took her a few seconds longer than he figured it would. Being devious did not come easily to the denizens of the sixty-fourth century. But she got there eventually, a crooked smile breaking out on her lips.

"If we can mimic their token, we can have access to the spire. And . . ."

"And arrest Pocus and Kadabra."

Citizen Hefa nodded crisply, all business. She gestured with her hands, and to Barry's astonishment, a hologram appeared there—a three-dimensional, full-color, perfectly proportioned 1:6 scale replica of the moment they'd just witnessed: Citizen Ali at the door to the magicians' spire.

Before he could ask how this was possible, Citizen Hefa anticipated his question. "Tachyonic replication technology," she said. "Crime scenes are logged for replay automatically by nanotech in my helmet."

Awesome. Barry's job as a CSI—not to mention Joe's as a detective—would be infinitely easier with this kind of tech at their disposal.

Which made him remember: His job as a CSI was in jeopardy. He needed to wrap things up here in the future and get back to his present.

Citizen Hefa's fingers fluttered, and the hologram scrolled forward. Citizen Ali rummaged, pulled something out of his pocket, held it up . . . The door opened.

"Can we zoom in on his hand?" Barry asked. "Get a better angle?"

Three of Citizen Hefa's fingers jiggled in a brief, complex pattern. The hologram sizzled and spat sparks, rotating so that Barry would have a clear view of the palm of Citizen Ali's hand when he raised it with his token. The hologram settled back into place and began to run again. Citizen Ali rummaged . . . held it up . . .

Barry stared. No. Impossible.

"Do it again," he heard himself whisper.

She ran the hologram again. Barry watched more closely this time. No. No *way.*

"I don't recognize it," Citizen Hefa said, squinting into the space between her own hands. "It seems to be completely flat, almost two-dimensional, with an image of some sort on it . . . Does it look familiar to you?"

It did. It looked *very* familiar to Barry. So familiar, in fact, that his stomach heaved and lurched with the impossibility of it. His brain rejected it. This simply *could not be happening.*

"Yeah," he whispered. "I know what it is. I have one."

Citizen Hefa did a double take. "Truly? You would not front, would you, homie?"

Swallowing hard, Barry felt for the concealed pocket in the tunic of his costume. It took only a moment to locate and withdraw the item he'd tucked within.

Millennia ago, he'd taken Madame Xanadu's mysterious playing card from Iris's desk and put it in his pocket. Now, millennia later, he knew what it was for.

"It's a key," he said in wonderment, holding it aloft for Citizen Hefa to see. "It unlocks the magicians' spire."

Had Madame Xanadu foreseen this moment? Barry wondered. From her storefront on the Central City Pier in the twenty-first century, had she peered forward into the future, navigating the web of alternate futures and worlds that might-yet-be to see this exact, specific moment in time, when he would need this card? And then had she neglected to scoop the card back into her deck so that Barry would take it with him . . .

. . . and leave it with Iris when he went to Earth 27 . . .

. . . so that it would still be intact when he needed it . . . ?

Had the whole thing been planned from the beginning? From the moment he'd stepped into Madame Xanadu's shop, had his free will been tossed out the window, replaced with . . . *fate*?

Was it truly magic?

Or was it just dumb luck?

Maybe, he thought, they were the same thing. And maybe, he thought further, it just didn't matter. He'd put one foot in front of the other, over and over again, running his path. Whether the path was newly made or predetermined, it had gotten him here, to this moment in time. To a world thousands of years after his own death, so far in the future that his name should be forgotten, crumbled to dust and scattered to history's winds.

And yet Citizen Hefa knew who he was. His story began in the past but resonated into the far, far future. Who could say what was intended and what happened by accident? In five thousand years, almost anything could happen. And apparently, almost anything had.

"This is our way in," he said, holding up the card. "I can't explain how or why, but I have it. And I'll use it."

Citizen Hefa clenched her fists briefly, and the hologram disappeared. "Let's go, Flash."

He shook his head. "No. It has to be me. Alone." He wasn't sure why, but he *was* sure. He had to brace the magicians in their den by himself. Maybe just to face down Hocus Pocus and finally throw off the shackles of fear and self-recrimination that he'd been bound up in ever since Hocus Pocus had mind-controlled him. Some part of him was still afraid, still living in fear that he could once again lose control of himself, find himself in a position where he not only couldn't help people but also couldn't stop himself from hurting them.

He had to face that fear, in the person of Hocus Pocus. He had to face it down and defeat it, once and for all.

"I'll go in," Barry told her, "and I'll bring them out."

Citizen Hefa hesitated, but Barry knew that she would agree. The Quantum Police might do a great job policing matter and energy, but their criminal-law-enforcement chops were atrophied. And she knew it. She would defer to the caveman from ancient history because he knew that the best way to stop the magicians wasn't by decommissioning their spire—it was by socking them in the jaw. Sometimes more than once, if you were lucky.

"I'll set up a dampening field outside the spire," Citizen Hefa said resolutely. "If any of them come through the door, it will prevent them from teleporting away immediately."

He grinned at her. "See? That's called backup in my time. Good one." He held up the card. "Can you scan this? And if something happens in there, can you—"

"—create a copy so that the Quantum Police can breach the door and offer assistance? Yes, of course. It's already done."

Since he hadn't noticed anything happen, he had to take her word for it. She must have sensed his skeptical hesitation, because she gestured with one hand, and an exact replica of the playing card appeared in her hand. It was, he had to admit, a great card trick.

"Voila!" he said, since she didn't.

"Voikitlakit may actually be inside," she warned him. "Be careful; she is quite dangerous."

Of *course* there was a techno-magician named *Voila*. Of course there was.

Barry gave Citizen Hefa a moment to set up her dampening field, and then he dashed to the front door. There was actually a doorknob there, and a great wave of homesickness washed over him at the sight of it.

A peephole set into the middle of the door made a slight clicking sound, and something telescoped from it, a lens protruding out perhaps an inch. Barry held up the card, its face toward the peephole, and sucked in an expectant breath.

It took no time at all. The peephole/telescope retreated flush to the door again, the knob turned on its own, and the door creaked open with a sound that told him it was the first thing in centuries that needed to be oiled.

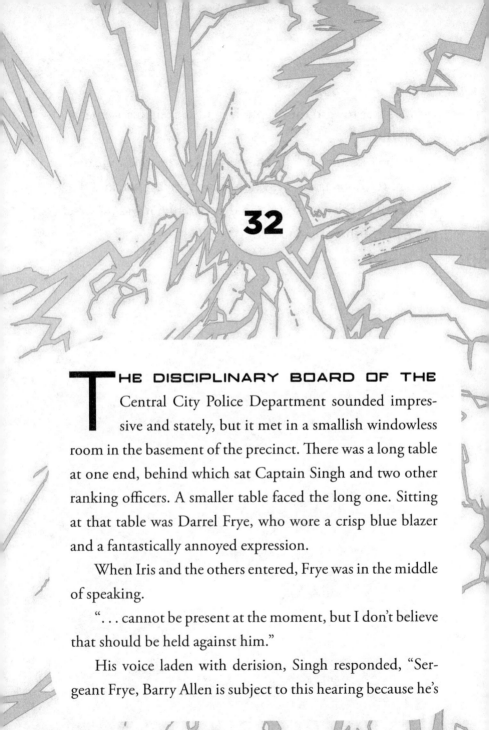

32

THE DISCIPLINARY BOARD OF THE Central City Police Department sounded impressive and stately, but it met in a smallish windowless room in the basement of the precinct. There was a long table at one end, behind which sat Captain Singh and two other ranking officers. A smaller table faced the long one. Sitting at that table was Darrel Frye, who wore a crisp blue blazer and a fantastically annoyed expression.

When Iris and the others entered, Frye was in the middle of speaking.

"... cannot be present at the moment, but I don't believe that should be held against him."

His voice laden with derision, Singh responded, "Sergeant Frye, Barry Allen is subject to this hearing because he's late to everything and rarely shows up when needed. If he can't even make it to his own *hearing*, that tells us everything we need to know!"

"Excuse me!" Iris said. "I'd like to speak on Barry Allen's behalf."

Frye turned in his chair to behold Iris, Joe, Cisco, Caitlin, and H.R. clustered just inside the door. He sighed, passed a hand over his eyes, and slumped a bit in his chair.

"Ms. West, this is highly irregular," Singh said. There was a microphone in front of him, and he put his hand over it. "Joe," he stage-whispered, "knock this off, and get this gaggle out of here!"

"Can't do it, Captain," Joe said. "You know that. We have to fight for Barry."

"When he isn't even here to fight for himself?"

"Especially then," Iris said.

One of the two officers on the board with Singh cleared her throat and spoke directly into her microphone. "There's no rule saying witnesses can't speak on behalf of the officer being disciplined if the officer isn't present," she said. "If Sergeant Frye would like to call these folks, I don't see why this board wouldn't at least give them the courtesy of hearing them out."

Frye started to groan, thought better of it, and turned it into a cough. He pointed to Iris. "You first, I guess."

Iris took a deep breath.

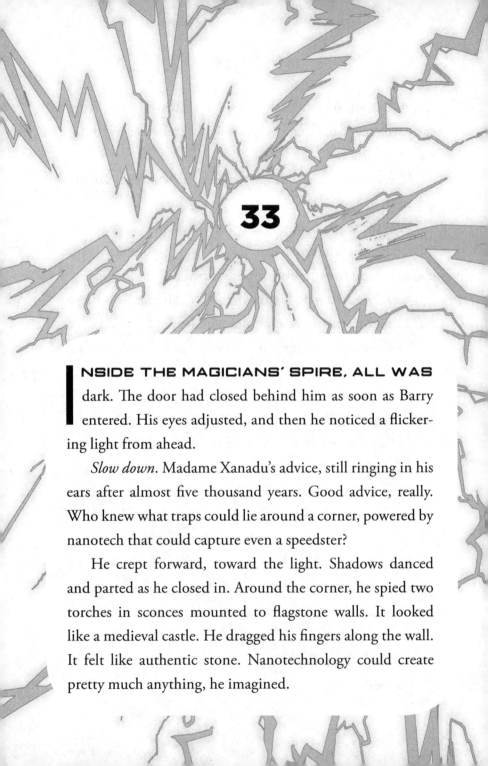

33

INSIDE THE MAGICIANS' SPIRE, ALL WAS dark. The door had closed behind him as soon as Barry entered. His eyes adjusted, and then he noticed a flickering light from ahead.

Slow down. Madame Xanadu's advice, still ringing in his ears after almost five thousand years. Good advice, really. Who knew what traps could lie around a corner, powered by nanotech that could capture even a speedster?

He crept forward, toward the light. Shadows danced and parted as he closed in. Around the corner, he spied two torches in sconces mounted to flagstone walls. It looked like a medieval castle. He dragged his fingers along the wall. It felt like authentic stone. Nanotechnology could create pretty much anything, he imagined.

"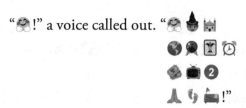!" a voice called out. "!"

At that, more torches spontaneously lit along the wall, bringing light to the darkened stone corridor. Barry followed them. He had no choice: The hallway only went in one direction, with no side corridors.

After a few moments, the corridor opened up to a massive theater. It looked like something from the late nineteenth century, with rich, sumptuous crimson curtains hanging over the stage, a gilded crystal chandelier suspended from the ceiling, and chairs set up bleacher-style, facing a proscenium arch and the stage itself. Another spasm of homesickness hit Barry. It was old to his twenty-first-century eyes but still familiar. Joe had dragged Iris and him to many a play at the Central City Municipal Theater when they were kids. This place looked like it.

Down on the stage, four figures stood, arguing. Barry immediately recognized Pocus and Kadabra, as well as the chunky man Citizen Hefa had identified as Citizen Ali. The fourth person was a woman, wearing an abbreviated outfit of coat and tails, along with a tall top hat perched at a rakish angle on her head.

Hello, Voila, Barry thought.

Four of them. Four magicians. As far as he knew, they all had the same powers and abilities as Hocus Pocus and Abra Kadabra. The last time he'd taken on a techno-magician, he'd had Wally's help and the backup of Team Flash at his disposal. Now he was going up against four of them on his own.

This doesn't end well for anyone, he thought mordantly.

They were speaking in raised voices, clearly distraught and annoyed with one another. Beyond that, he couldn't nail down specifics—they were speaking in that strange sixty-fourth-century language that he did not understand. He should have asked Citizen Hefa to download *that* into *his* Wernicke's area.

Crouching behind the last row of seats, concealed by shadows, he peered down onto the stage. Speed and surprise were his advantages, of course, and he could—

Whoa !

As he watched and pondered his best course of action, Hocus Pocus suddenly spun around and lashed out with his wand, sending a beam of light at Citizen Ali, who reacted a split second too late, raising his own wand in an effort to deflect.

The beam of light exploded into a shower of multicolored sparks and flares. Citizen Ali fell back several steps, waving his wand madly. Little clouds appeared, firing bolts of lightning.

Meanwhile, Voila floated up into the air and fired a blast of frigid air at Abra Kadabra, who made a gesture with his left hand that redirected the cold beam up into the rafters. It started snowing inside, big fat flakes drifting down from the shadows up above.

Barry shuddered, remembering his fight with Hocus Pocus in the Central City Park. The magician had made trees come to life, conjured a waterspout from a fountain, and reversed gravity. Now there were four of them with those kinds of powers, apparently ready to kill one another.

At least they're isolated in this spire. They can't hurt anyone else in here.

A stray lightning bolt from one of Citizen Ali's clouds zipped right over Barry's head and exploded against the wall behind him. *OK, strike that—they can't hurt anyone but* me!

He peeked over the chair again. Someone had conjured an enormous bullfrog, which now squatted in the center of the stage, lashing out with its tongue at Citizen Ali. Hocus Pocus was floating in the air with Voila, the two of them concentrating their firepower on Abra Kadabra, who was down on one knee, teeth gritted in concentration as he gestured manically, sending lightning bolts, bursts of flame, freeze rays, and other harmful blasts scattering off in all directions.

It was a coup. Voila and Pocus were trying to get rid of Kadabra. And then, no doubt, Pocus would betray Voila.

After all, he wanted to be the Most Exalted Abra Kadabra himself, and he wouldn't let anything stand in his way.

Barry was tempted to let them fight it out among themselves and then take out the winner on his own. But they didn't seem to be pulling their punches, and he couldn't just stand by (well, crouch by) and watch people get killed. Not even evil techno-magicians from the sixty-fourth century.

He heard Cisco's voice in his head: *You know, if you'd lay off the morals for just five seconds, you'd make your life a lot easier.*

And then he heard Joe: *That's not the man I raised, Cisco.*

And then Iris: *It's a good thing we know you're kidding, Cisco. Barry would never do that.*

And he wouldn't. With a sigh, he popped up from behind the seats and raced down the aisle toward the feuding wizards.

First, he extricated Citizen Ali from the bullfrog's tongue. It was a sticky, slimy business, and he was glad that his costume had gloves. The bullfrog croaked in indignation and hopped into the air, shooting its tongue out at Barry at the same time.

And now the wizards were aware that the Flash was on the scene.

"Flash!" Hocus Pocus screamed.

"Flash!" bellowed Abra Kadabra.

"💩!" said Voila.

Citizen Ali said nothing. He was furiously pawing at himself, trying to wipe off the coating of frog saliva that had covered his entire midsection.

Kadabra snapped his fingers. Large spotlights wrenched themselves free from the ceiling and spun through the air. One of them collided with Voila, knocking her back down to the floor. Pocus managed to dodge another.

A third came right for Barry. He avoided it, but as it sailed past him, its cable snaked out and wrapped around his ankles, tripping him. He landed with a w*hoof!* on the floor, and the spotlight spun around, a mouth suddenly opening where the bulb was. The glass became teeth, shining brightly, and the thing shot over to him, its maw wide.

Watching the spotlight-turned-monster zip toward him, glass teeth gnashing, Barry thought, *Well*, there's *something you don't see every day.*

Above, Hocus Pocus sent a flurry of flaming hail down toward Barry and Abra Kadabra. Voila, meanwhile, had pulled something like ten yards of silk out of her shirt-sleeve and sent it flapping and flailing through the air until it wrapped around Citizen Ali, who was still sloughing off bullfrog spit. The silk enveloped him from head to toe and started squeezing.

Barry managed to get to his knees. The spotlight grew closer, its cable tugging Barry in toward those hideous, gleaming teeth. He put his palms on the floor and started vibrating. In a moment, the spotlight trembled, then blurred as the vibrations really took hold. An instant later, the teeth shattered into glass dust, and a puff of smoke went up from the innards of the spotlight. The cable went slack around Barry's ankles.

I just killed an inanimate object. Achievement unlocked.

Dodging the fiery hail and random spurts of laser energy from Kadabra, Barry weaved his way across the stage to Citizen Ali, whose face had gone purple and whose eyes bugged out as the cloth constricted around him. Voila was playing for keeps.

Barry grabbed the dangling end of the silk. It thrashed in his hands and tried to wrap itself around his wrist, but he turned his hand this way and that to foil its attempt. Then he ran counterclockwise around Citizen Ali, unraveling the fabric as he went. In the next instant, he snapped the cloth like a bullwhip, spun it over his head, and sent it sailing through the air at Voila.

She saw it coming and had just enough time to shout something he didn't understand but that was probably not terribly nice. The silk enwrapped her and squeezed. Voila dropped out of the air . . .

. . . and landed right on top of Citizen Ali. *Clonk!* Both of them were out cold.

"You imbecile!" Hocus Pocus shouted from above. "You're interfering with matters that do not concern you!"

"Once I've dealt with this pretender," Kadabra snarled, indicating Pocus, "I'll allow myself the pleasure of killing *you*."

"I'm glad you guys speak ancient English," Barry told them. "Makes it more fun to do the whole hero/villain banter thing."

"Banter this!" Kadabra made a wide, broad gesture with both hands, swinging his arms out to his sides and snapping his fingers at the same time. Barry charged toward him, but just then the room shook around him. Suddenly, the walls pulled away, twisted, turned, and reconfigured themselves into a ceiling and floor. The audience seating area bent and flipped as if on a massive hinge, the aisle stairs now turned ninety degrees. The entire theater contorted itself into something out of the mind of M. C. Escher.

Gravity had gone wonky, too. Hocus Pocus alighted on what had been the floor but was now a wall, set at a ninety-degree angle to where Barry stood. Kadabra was a few yards away, snarling with satisfaction. He pushed out with his hands, and two fireballs soared at Barry, who ducked and then ran sideways along a set of stairs that now led right into a corner.

The fireballs were following him. At the corner, he juked left, now running upside-down along what had been a wall a few seconds ago. "Above" his head—but actually under him—he saw Hocus Pocus swing his wand wildly. A slick of ice appeared under Barry's feet, and he skidded out of control along the "ceiling," until gravity suddenly decided to do its job again, and he found himself dropping like a stone.

The bullfrog, meanwhile, had become so disoriented by the reconfiguration of the room that it hopped straight up, hit a perpendicular line of new gravity, and ended up speeding right at Barry, its tongue flapping in the wind, flecks of spittle spattering everywhere.

Just as the bullfrog reached him, it croaked loudly in his ear, deafening him for a moment. He lashed out at it, knocking it away as he plunged downward. The bullfrog croaked again in outrage and "fell" upward to land on the wall/ceiling.

Barry, though, kept falling down. He recovered from the explosive *croak* in his ear at the last second and spun his arms in a whirlwind. He was too late; he created a cushion of air to land on but not one deep enough. The impact of hitting the floor rattled his bones and knocked the wind out of him.

Gasping for breath, he tried to push himself onto his knees but couldn't move. His eyes watered with the pain. *Get up!* he told himself. *There's two magicians and a bullfrog on your butt! Get up!*

Two feet came into view before him. The room tilted again, all topsy-turvy, and Barry tumbled down an incline, crashing into a breathless heap on what had been the floor and was now a wall. The feet followed him, ignoring the rejiggered gravity. He looked up.

It was Abra Kadabra, looming over him, leering, stroking his beard.

"Now, Flash," he said with glee, "I will fulfill both of our destinies! I always knew that when you vanished from history, it had to be because *I*, your greatest foe, had lured you to the future and killed you here and now, in a time when your precious friends could not even find your body, much less save you."

Get up! He's serious!

Barry pushed hard on the floor but couldn't move in time. Abra Kadabra's fingers danced in the air, powerful pulses of light building between them, and then—

And then Kadabra made a sound that was a little *Urk!* and collapsed, unconscious.

This wasn't the good news Barry had been hoping for. Standing right behind Kadabra was none other than Hocus Pocus, a deadly, satisfied gleam in his eye, holding a large hammer that he'd just used to bash Kadabra in the back of the head.

"Not terribly sophisticated," he admitted, "but it got the job done. Now *I* am truly the Most Exalted! I am Abra

Kadabra, and *I* will be the one history records as having defeated the Flash!"

The hammer disappeared, and the wand materialized in his hand. He drew a complicated pattern in the air and pointed the wand at Barry.

Barry rolled to one side just in time. The beam missed him by mere centimeters. He cast a panicked look over his shoulder and saw the light of madness and jubilation in Hocus Pocus's eyes. And something else. He saw something else, too, and he crossed his fingers . . .

"Die, speed freak!" Pocus screamed, and he reared back with the wand.

Just at that instant, the giant bullfrog—having hit a wall and propelled itself away with its massively powerful hind legs—came hurtling through the air and collided with Hocus Pocus, knocking him off balance and sending him staggering off to the left.

It was just the break Barry needed. He drew in a deep breath and picked himself up off the ground. *Let's hear it for* Rana catesbeiana*!* he thought, sending a cheerful thought toward the bullfrog. *Ribbit, big guy!*

He stumbled at first as the room lurched again, then found his feet. Pocus was screaming his aggravation, wrestling with the bullfrog, but then he just gave up and waved his wand. In a burst of color and smoke, the bullfrog blinked out of existence.

Barry charged at Pocus, who seethed. "Flash!" he yelled. "Suffer the wrath of Abra Kadabra!"

Bam! An explosion of colors erupted from Pocus's wand. Barry held up his hands to shield his eyes as bright, blinding hues burst before him. His speed carried him through the riot of tints and tinctures, right to Hocus Pocus.

"You're no Abra Kadabra," Barry said, throwing out a fist. "You're just Hocus Pocus."

His punch caught Pocus in the gut. The magician exhaled a very satisfying, injured *Whuff!* sound and doubled over in pain.

As Pocus sank to his knees before him, Barry drew back his fist to hit him a second time. Just then, the room decided to reconfigure itself yet again, and gravity slid out from underneath Barry, sending him in a free fall to his left, where he fell into the wall.

Perpendicular to Barry, Hocus Pocus coughed once and got to his feet, shaking only slightly. "Once I've ended you, Flash, no one will doubt my supremacy. I will be the one true Abra Kadabra, for all time!"

He thrust the wand before him, and a beam of light shot out. Barry thought he recognized that beam of light, and when it struck the floor harmlessly as he sidestepped it, he knew he was right: It was the same mind-control energy that Pocus had originally zapped him with back in the twenty-first century.

Chills ran up and down Barry's spine, like a fleet of mini-Flashes wearing boots made of ice. He couldn't let that happen again.

"This time, I won't make the mistake of letting you run around on your own!" Pocus howled, firing off another beam. Barry dodged it but just barely. He was still breathing hard from his fall, and the room's shift of configuration and gravity had his head spinning.

Just then, Pocus launched another volley of lights, spinning, pulsating blobs of color that disoriented him further. He swung his arms around, batting them away. They broke apart like soap bubbles and changed colors, making it even more difficult to see.

Fine, then. Top speed.

He vibrated his arms, karate-chopping through the air before him. Big bubbles split into smaller bubbles, which split into even smaller bubbles, the air awash in blinking, flashing blobs of color. After a few seconds, a path began to clear, and the air before him went shimmery with the after-image of his own vibrating hands slashing and chopping.

As an open channel formed, a new sight swam into view: Hocus Pocus, standing directly before him, his wand pointed and already aglow with power.

Zap! Before Barry could move or react, the beam struck him.

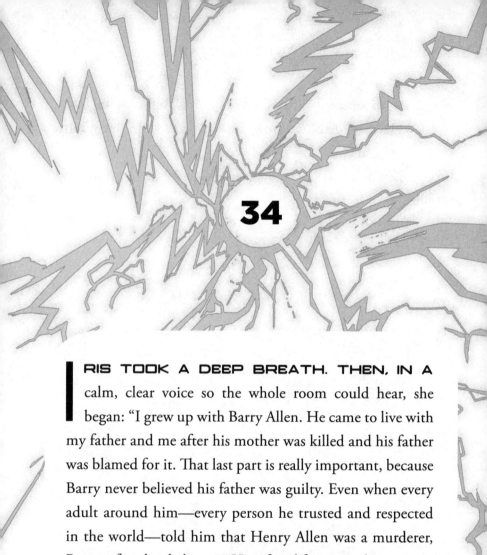

34

RIS TOOK A DEEP BREATH. THEN, IN A calm, clear voice so the whole room could hear, she began: "I grew up with Barry Allen. He came to live with my father and me after his mother was killed and his father was blamed for it. That last part is really important, because Barry never believed his father was guilty. Even when every adult around him—every person he trusted and respected in the world—told him that Henry Allen was a murderer, Barry refused to believe it. He refused for more than twenty years, and then he proved that Henry Allen was innocent.

"You can't throw away that kind of dogged determination. You can't discard someone who possesses such a penetrating eye. Barry's job is to find the evidence that helps the police prove guilt or innocence. His own life story proves that there is no one better."

35

NO! BARRY'S HEART HAMMERED
impossibly fast, even for the Flash. *No! Not again!*

But it was happening. Already, he felt the
familiar, nauseating sensation of Hocus Pocus's nanites in
his brain, compelling him to do as he was ordered.

"Stay right there," Pocus said, grinning. "And when I say
stay right there, I mean no vibrating, either. Don't move from
that spot."

Barry tried to move forward, backward, to one side . . .
Nothing. His mind screamed for his legs to obey, but his limbs
would only listen to Hocus Pocus now. He stood rooted to the
spot as though he'd put down a taproot in soil.

Hocus Pocus straightened his spine and tilted his head
to one side, then the other, cracking his neck. A vicious,
sadistic grin split his features. "Oh, Flash." His voice ran

like rancid honey. "Did you truly think that you could come here to my era and cross my path and walk away whole?"

"Do whatever you like to me, Hocus Pocus. You'll still never be Abra Kadabra." Maybe if he taunted Pocus, he could get him to slip up.

Pocus bristled. "You have no say in that, you caveman interloper! Only the techno-magicians can determine who is Abra Kadabra, and *I* am the last techno-magician standing!"

Barry cut his eyes to the left, where Abra Kadabra lay in a crumpled heap. There would be no help coming from that direction . . . and he wasn't sure he wanted that kind of help, anyway. Hocus Pocus was nuts, but Abra Kadabra seemed to enjoy causing pain. There was no good way out of this.

Think fast, Barry told himself. As Hocus Pocus strode to him, he thought, *Think faster!*

The magician stopped a few inches from Barry. He reached out and pulled Barry's cowl down. "There. I want to be looking into your eyes when I end you."

"You've already been beaten," Barry said. "The Quantum Police are waiting for you. Unless you plan to spend the rest of your life in this spire, you'll have to go outside eventually. And they'll take you down. You and your goofy, antiquated friends. You're all gonna spend a long, long time floating in a stasis cell."

"*Goofy, antiquated?*" Pocus seethed through clenched teeth. "I am a master magician of the highest order! I am Abra Kadabra!"

At this point, all Barry could do was stall for time and hope for the best. And Hocus Pocus was such a glory hound that mocking his wizardry was the easiest way to keep him talking. Maybe Citizen Ali would wake up. Maybe Kadabra and Pocus would kill each other. Maybe the Quantum Police would finally decide to barge in.

Probably none of those things would happen. But Barry had to try.

"A master magician of the highest order?" Barry huffed sarcastically. "Please. Anyone in the sixty-fourth century can do the things you do. I watched a hundred people disappear on their own. I watched Citizen Hefa conjure a Coke from thin air. Good one, too."

"Charlatans!" Pocus roared, so angry that flecks of spittle flew out of his mouth. "Mockeries! They have no sense of pageantry! No sense of drama! Dull little cretins, living dull little lives."

With that, Pocus kicked the supine form of Abra Kadabra and passed his wand over him. Even unconscious, Kadabra began to tremble and moan in pain. As Barry watched, a pale mist rose from Kadabra's pores and hovered in the air.

"What are you doing?" Barry demanded as Kadabra shook and groaned. "You're killing him!"

"Hardly," said Pocus. "I want him alive to witness my ultimate triumph. I'm just stripping the smarttech from his bloodstream. He once called me a fool for putting most of my power into my wand. Now who's the fool?"

Kadabra cried out with one final expulsion of agony, and then his eyes flew open as the mist around him dissipated.

"What have you done?" he whispered, gazing up at Hocus Pocus.

"Who am I?" Pocus asked, pointing his wand threateningly.

Kadabra gritted his teeth and flexed his fingers . . . but nothing happened. A long moment passed, and then he hung his head.

"You are the Most Exalted Abra Kadabra," he said in a whisper.

"And who are you?"

"I am no one."

The new Abra Kadabra threw back his head and howled with mocking, harsh laughter. He tapped the man who was now no one on his head and watched as a series of overlapping chains appeared from nowhere, wrapping around and securing "no one" and then dragging him off behind the stage curtain.

Abra Kadabra turned back to Barry. "And now, Flash, it is *your* turn. History records that you vanished into a great Crisis in the year 2024."

"Tell me something I don't know."

"Well, far be it from me to argue with history. I will return to your time and masquerade as you. No one will ever know. Your friends, your family . . . They will all think I am you, and when the moment is right, before I disappear forever . . . I will crush them all. Think on that."

Barry strained mightily to move, even a millimeter, but Kadabra's control was solid and strong. He tried to vibrate, but he'd been commanded not to.

"You'd better kill me, then," he said with complete seriousness. "Because otherwise I *will* find a way to get to you. Threaten me, fine. Threaten *them*, and—"

"Oh, shut up!" Kadabra took a few steps back. "I've decided your fate. When we clashed in your area, I commandeered your mind and made you my puppet. Figuratively speaking. Now, I shall do so *literally*." His lips twisted into a cruel, sly smile. "I'm going to turn you into an actual puppet, and I will pull your strings whenever I like!"

Barry almost laughed, but he could see that Kadabra was dead serious. Was that even possible? To turn a human being into a puppet?

It's the ol' reverse Pinocchio, he heard Cisco say in his

head. *Anything's possible with the kind of nanotech at his disposal.*

Reverse gravity . . . Conjure matter from thin air . . . Transmute flesh and blood into wood and fabric.

"You're insane," Barry told him. *Stall. Stall! The Quantum Police could be heading here right now!*

"Sanity is an outdated notion," Kadabra said. "When the building blocks of reality are at your fingertips, what is *sane* and what is not no longer matter."

"So, what, now you call yourself Abra Kadabra, and you suddenly get the keys to the car and all of the other guy's money? That's what this is all about?"

"I don't expect a primitive like you to understand," Kadabra sneered. "Suffice it to say, I am now more powerful than I ever could have been as Hocus Pocus. I have subsumed my old master and taken his abilities as my own. But that isn't the best part, Flash."

"Tell me." *Keep stalling.*

Kadabra grinned. "History records that the Flash's greatest foe went by the name Abra Kadabra. And now that is— and always will be—me!" He took one more step back and brandished his wand. "Now, prepare yourself, Flash. You will see a beam of light and then . . . Well, and then it will be over."

Beam of light, Barry thought. *Beam of light . . .*

A bead of sweat ran down his scalp, to his temple, then down his cheek.

Zap! Kadabra thrust his wand forward.

Barry had been ordered to stay where he stood and not to vibrate, but he still had superspeed, and his perceptions were still superfast. He watched the beam of light as it raced toward him.

Beam of light. Beam of light. What can I do?

And then it hit him. With mere microseconds left, he realized what he had to do.

He had to stand in the same spot and remain solid, but Kadabra hadn't ordered not to move *at all*. He could obey Kadabra's commands and still do something.

So he turned in place, spinning around and around like a top, at the absolute fastest speed he could muster. Electricity crackled and arced around his body, generating heat. Tremendous heat.

He kept spinning, and he hoped it was enough.

The beam of light reached him. It passed through the zone of superheated air around him.

And just as the incredibly hot air above summertime street pavement can warp light enough to cause what appear to be ripples, the superhot air around Barry *bent* the beam of light coming from Abra Kadabra's wand.

It was called the refractive effect. It was science, and it was a Flash Fact.

The beam bent all the way *around* Barry and spit itself back at Abra Kadabra, who had many powers and abilities, but superspeed was not one of them. He had just enough time to gasp and move his wand slightly before the beam of light struck him full on.

Barry stopped spinning and wobbled dizzily, almost falling over. "Didn't anybody ever tell you that heat bends light?" he asked.

There was no answer from Abra Kadabra, who had collapsed into a jumbled heap of white tuxedo and cloak. Barry found that he was free to move, the surest sign that he'd beaten Kadabra.

He shook off his paralysis and walked over to Kadabra. Still no movement from the magician.

I didn't want to kill *him* . . .

Barry kicked the wand away from Kadabra's hand and crouched down. There was something off . . .

He noticed strings tangled together atop Kadabra's cloak. When he unraveled them, he discovered that they were tied to the bars of a wooden cross. As he pulled at the cross, the strings tautened and pulled Kadabra upright.

Abra Kadabra was a puppet. A marionette, to be exact. His face was made of felt, his hands stubby, blunt chunks of wood. His hinged jaw hung open, and his eyes were painted dots.

Barry twisted the wooden cross. Kadabra's left hand jerked, and his jaw clacked shut. "Flash!" he said in a high-pitched voice.

Once more, Barry manipulated the cross. Kadabra's jaw moved again. "What have you done to me?"

"In my time, it was called *poetic justice*," Barry told him. He jostled the cross and made Abra Kadabra dance a little jig. "You are now the Most Exalted and Wooden Abra Kadabra. Enjoy."

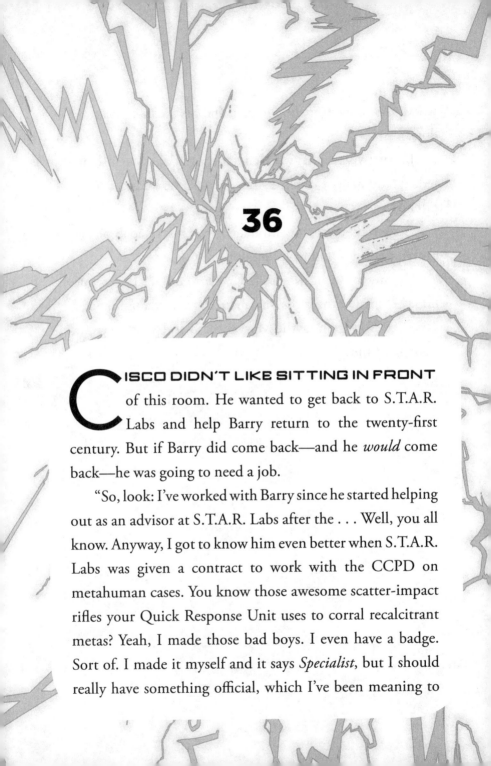

36

CISCO DIDN'T LIKE SITTING IN FRONT
of this room. He wanted to get back to S.T.A.R.
Labs and help Barry return to the twenty-first
century. But if Barry did come back—and he *would* come
back—he was going to need a job.

"So, look: I've worked with Barry since he started helping
out as an advisor at S.T.A.R. Labs after the . . . Well, you all
know. Anyway, I got to know him even better when S.T.A.R.
Labs was given a contract to work with the CCPD on
metahuman cases. You know those awesome scatter-impact
rifles your Quick Response Unit uses to corral recalcitrant
metas? Yeah, I made those bad boys. I even have a badge.
Sort of. I made it myself and it says *Specialist*, but I should
really have something official, which I've been meaning to

talk to someone about, but I can see by your expressions that perhaps this is neither the time nor the place, and so . . .

"Barry Allen's a good egg. Which . . . I don't know why we call people good eggs and bad eggs, but Barry Allen is one of those organic, cage-free brown eggs with a double yolk, you know? You get a nice omelet with Barry Allen, is what I'm saying. My boy doesn't play around. He kicks butt when there is butt begging to be kicked, and he dials it down when it's time to be chill and let things slide. He groks people. He's like Spock, if Spock got down and boogied. He's also got some Kirk and Bones in him, not to mention some Sulu and . . . You know what? He's the whole bridge crew, OK? That's the guy we're talking about. He could fly the *Enterprise* solo, which makes me think of Han Solo, and, yeah, Barry's a little bit Jedi, too, in his own way. Jedi. Starfleet. I'm just saying: You don't toss out a guy like that.

"Who do I talk to about my badge again?"

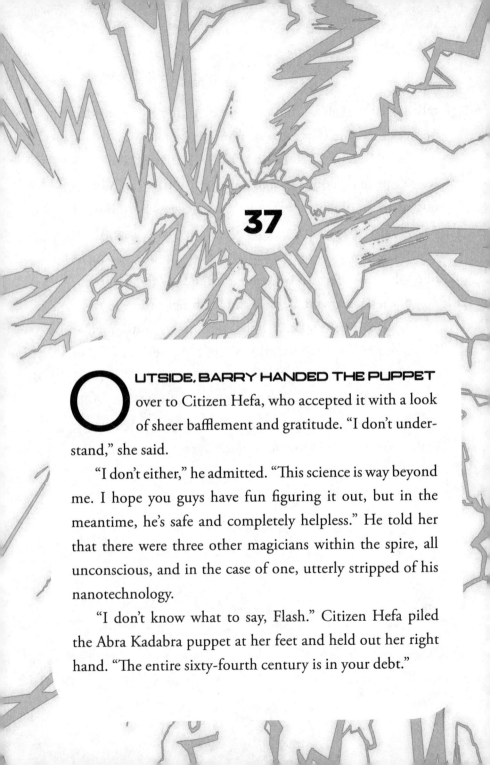

37

OUTSIDE, BARRY HANDED THE PUPPET over to Citizen Hefa, who accepted it with a look of sheer bafflement and gratitude. "I don't understand," she said.

"I don't either," he admitted. "This science is way beyond me. I hope you guys have fun figuring it out, but in the meantime, he's safe and completely helpless." He told her that there were three other magicians within the spire, all unconscious, and in the case of one, utterly stripped of his nanotechnology.

"I don't know what to say, Flash." Citizen Hefa piled the Abra Kadabra puppet at her feet and held out her right hand. "The entire sixty-fourth century is in your debt."

Barry shook her hand and grinned. "Don't worry about it. All in a day's work for a time-traveling super-speedster. Speaking of which . . . It's time for me to relax my internal vibrations and return to my time."

"I hope you have not missed out on anything important while you were gone, Flash."

He cocked his head. "Missed out? What do you mean? I'm going to return one second after I left. I won't have missed anything."

Citizen Hefa's eyes widened. "Oh, no, Flash. You won't return one second after you left the twenty-first century. It doesn't work that way."

"What do you mean?" he asked again. A cold feeling clamped around his heart. "What. Do. You. Mean?"

Citizen Hefa spread her hands helplessly and searched for the right words. "When you return to your era, it will be at a point at which all the time you spent in your future has passed. Otherwise, you would be out of harmony with the rest of the universe."

"What?" That didn't sound good. The cold intensified.

She gnawed at her lower lip, again searching for words. "Imagine that you travel to the future and spend twenty-four hours there. If you returned to your present at the moment at which you left, *you* would be twenty-four hours older than everything else in the entire universe. Your atoms and molecules would be out of sync with the rest of reality. The internal vibrations you've maintained thanks to the Cosmic Treadmill act as a sort of clock, keeping you in pace with your own time period. When you relax them, you return to the appropriate moment in time."

"But . . ." Barry stammered, "I've traveled to the past before and returned almost at the same moment, and nothing bad happened."

"How long were you in the past?"

He thought about the times he'd time-traveled before. Each time, he'd only been in the past a short time before returning to his own relative present.

Not like now. He'd been in the thirtieth century for several hours, then in the sixty-fourth century for even more time . . . He hadn't been keeping track. Because he didn't think it was necessary. But a *lot* of time had passed for him in the future! Which meant that he'd been missing for the same amount of time in his era.

Iris. Iris must be terrified. And Cisco and the others . . . They would probably be trying to find him, trying to figure out what had happened. So soon after being lost on Earth 27, to do this to them again . . .

The cold feeling around his heart became painful. He

had to leave. Right now. He couldn't make them wait a second longer.

"I have to go," he told Citizen Hefa. "Right now."

She nodded gravely in understanding, raising a hand in farewell. "I look forward to our next meeting, Flash," she said, and before he could ask what she meant by that, he'd already begun slipping away, fading into the time stream . . .

. . . and then fading back in almost before he realized it.

The S.T.A.R. Labs Cortex materialized around him, swimming into view like a mirage in the desert. Disoriented, he stumbled a few steps to his left, colliding with a chair. He steadied himself, then sank into the chair. *Whew!*

He was home.

The Cortex was empty and quiet. But on the floor was a large scorch mark that looked as if it had been somehow cut in half. Something had happened here while he was gone.

Barry wondered what time it was. For that matter, what *day* was it?

He scooted the chair over to one of the computers. Yikes! It was midday of the day *after* he'd left for the future! Which meant . . .

Which meant his hearing at CCPD was going on *right now!*

He had to change clothes and get to the hearing immediately. Maybe there was still time to save his job.

Before he could do anything, an alert sounded, and the computer screen lit up: PROCESS COMPLETE.

Barry scanned the screen quickly. Someone—Cisco, no doubt—had been running a lengthy process on the system, and it was now over. As best he could tell, it was identifying several spots in the Central City sewers.

Earthworm? he wondered.

There was a thick file nearby. Barry read through it at superspeed, going so fast that one sheet of paper actually burst into flame. He blew it out and kept reading. A whole five seconds passed.

In his absence, Team Flash had figured out the who, what, why, how, and when of Earthworm. And now the computer had just spit out six possibilities for the *where*.

Barry had a choice: Go to the hearing or confront Earthworm before he could kill again.

Actually, he had no choice at all. The answer was obvious. At top speed, he raced away from the Cortex and S.T.A.R. Labs.

38

CAITLIN SIGHED. THIS HEARING WAS so . . . boring. She couldn't imagine being a lawyer, listening to people drone on and on, wondering whom to believe. She worked in facts, science, something she could see in front of her. She took a deep breath. She was just going to have to give the facts now, give them something to believe in—and they *could* believe in Barry.

"I'm not just Barry Allen's personal physician and coworker; I'm also honored to call him a friend.

"Honored because I have never in my life met a man who so embodies the principles of justice, ethical behavior, and personal sacrifice. I have never once seen Barry put his own needs or wants ahead of someone else's. Has he been tempted? Sure. We're all tempted. But he makes the right choice, every single time.

"I know that Barry can be . . . I was going to say 'unreliable,' but that's just not true. Barry is steadfast and utterly reliable. He gets the job done. He may disappear for a while. He may be unreachable. This is a part of his process. His mind works in ways we can't totally understand.

"Maybe this will help: I once had a patient with chronic back pain that was spreading into both legs. Horrible, horrible pain. She couldn't stand for more than thirty seconds at a time. Sitting or lying down only dulled the pain. It was always there.

"By the time she came to me, she'd been to a chiropractor, an acupuncturist, and a physical therapist. I sent her in for an MRI and prescribed some meds. She asked me if she should keep seeing the other doctors who were working on her.

"I told her, 'Absolutely. Keep doing all of it. Between the four of us, one of us is going to fix this. We may never even know which one of us fixed you, but does it really matter? All that matters is, you won't be in pain anymore.'

"Barry's process is his process. Does it really matter how he gets the job done, as long as it's done?"

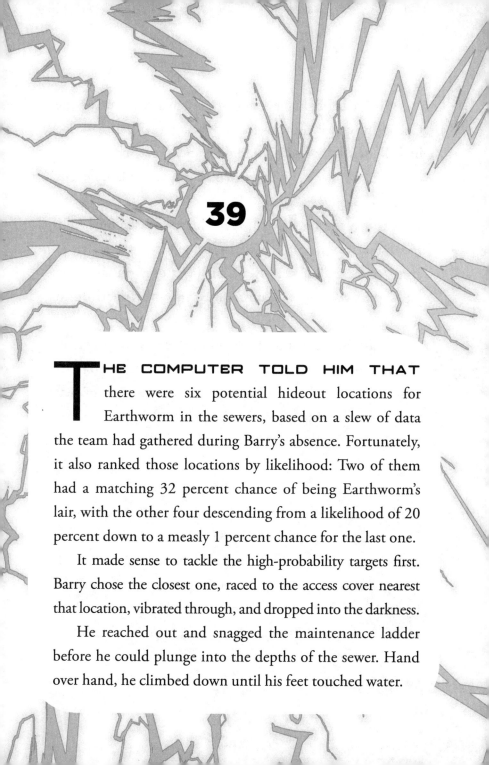

39

THE COMPUTER TOLD HIM THAT there were six potential hideout locations for Earthworm in the sewers, based on a slew of data the team had gathered during Barry's absence. Fortunately, it also ranked those locations by likelihood: Two of them had a matching 32 percent chance of being Earthworm's lair, with the other four descending from a likelihood of 20 percent down to a measly 1 percent chance for the last one.

It made sense to tackle the high-probability targets first. Barry chose the closest one, raced to the access cover nearest that location, vibrated through, and dropped into the darkness.

He reached out and snagged the maintenance ladder before he could plunge into the depths of the sewer. Hand over hand, he climbed down until his feet touched water.

With a penlight he'd grabbed on his way out of the Cortex, he checked the pages he'd brought with him. Cisco had thoughtfully had his program include a schematic of each area of the sewer that could be Earthworm's lair. Details counted. *Good job, Cisco.*

Barry made his way through the sewer carefully, fully aware that Earthworm could be lurking in any shadow or even on the ceiling. He swept his light over the dripping pipes, the sweating walls, down into the murky, debris-filled water.

At last, he made it to the spot indicated by the program.

And there was nothing there. Just an old electrical junction box that had been disconnected decades ago but that hung open, its hinges rusted and cracked with age.

OK, he thought, and he crossed off the location on his list. *One down.*

Wally could hardly sit still. His legs bounced up and down. He wanted to race around the room. He decided he'd better get this over with as quickly as possible. "I don't have much to say. I only met Barry recently. Turns out we're brothers, in a way. At first—I'll be honest—I didn't think much of him. But then I really got to know him. And I realized that, other than my dad, he's the best, most solid, most caring and giving man I've ever met. Just knowing him has made me want to be better, to improve myself, to do more for the world.

"I don't know what else to say, but I also kinda think that says it all."

Barry raced across the city to the second location on his list. He was aware that his disciplinary hearing was going on *right at that moment*. But it didn't really matter. Without him there, it had probably ended as soon as it began.

I'm not a cop anymore, he thought. And then he shook the thought away. He had something more important to focus on.

H.R. drained his coffee. He smiled as the caffeine took effect.

"As President Gore once said—"

"What?

"Oh, yes, of course I meant Vice President Gore.

"Anyway, I've lost my train of thought now. Barry Allen is an excellent compadre and a—what's the term?—a solid dude. Your Honors, I rest my case."

At the intersection of Kanigher and Waid, Barry zipped into traffic at invisible speed, then vibrated straight down through another access cover in the street. Grabbed another ladder. Climbed down again.

Once he had his feet under him on solid—though damp, dank, and smelly—ground, he consulted the printout for his directions. With his trusty flashlight leading the way, he maneuvered through the sewers until the map indicated that he was almost at the location in question. It was just a right turn, ducking under some pipes, then scrabbling through a partly concealed pipe.

Barry dropped to his hands and knees and crawled through the pipe. The filth around him turned his stomach, but he clamped down hard on his nausea. He had work to do.

Emerging from the pipe after a ten-yard crawl, Barry stood, vibrated for a moment to shake off the disgusting water like a dog shaking itself dry, then headed through a low arch into a larger chamber.

Bingo.

The chamber was twelve feet to a side and maybe twice as tall, its ceiling vanishing into darkness. A hospital bed, one leg broken and propped up with a cinder block, rested at one end of the room, with a makeshift IV stand nearby, along with an old, broken-down dresser on which lay a series of medical instruments. There were trash bags spilling out old clothing, some waterlogged boxes containing rags and more medical instruments, as well as bottles of rubbing alcohol and cotton pads. A makeshift surgery, if you didn't mind the bacteria and the filth of the sewers getting into your body.

And there, at the opposite end of the room, was Earthworm himself, hunched over one of the crates, rummaging through it with his back to Barry.

He was tall—six-three or -four to Barry's trained eye—but painfully thin. Maybe a hundred-thirty pounds at the most. Wasting away. His organs perpetually in a state of rot. His skin, sallow and the color of bad cheese. His every movement pained.

He was dying. According to what Team Flash had sussed out, the man had been dying ever since the particle accelerator explosion had turned Barry into the Flash.

Flip a coin. Roll the dice. Fly your kite in a lightning storm. Sometimes you're Ben Franklin. Sometimes you're Georg Wilhelm Richmann.

He felt sorry for the villain. He hadn't asked for this. Hadn't asked to find his only hope for survival in the reeking confines of the Central City sewers, clad in a threadbare black duster and a dull red scarf that was almost completely frayed apart.

He hadn't asked for this at all, and yet here they were. Hero and villain. A man who was living and a man who was dying.

Sensing something, Earthworm spun around. He hissed at Barry in outrage, clenching the hands at the ends of his spindly arms into fists.

"Go!" he shrieked in offended anger, and then he doubled over as a great coughing fit racked his body. His deterioration was accelerating. He was in terrible, terrible shape. "Go back to Upworld!"

"I can't do that," Barry told him. "I can't let you kill anyone else. It's over."

Barry sensed movement in the water around him, tiny currents eddying and colliding. Rats. Lots of them. Massing near him.

He stayed perfectly still and then raised one hand, holding it out palm up. Offering it as though in supplication.

"Dr. Hynde, I don't want to hurt you. You've harmed a great many people—killed some, even—but I know you did it out of desperation. Please, come with me, and let's put an end to this. Let's stop the killing. I can't promise to cure you, but I can promise you the very best minds will be working on your—"

Earthworm howled and launched himself at Barry. Barry sidestepped and rabbit-punched him at superspeed. Earthworm collapsed, unconscious, at his feet.

Barry sighed, dejected. "*Or* I could just punch you out. Why does it always have to be that way?"

Joe held his hands out at his sides and gave a slight shrug.

"You all know me. You know I don't mess around.

"I was more than the cop on the scene when Nora Allen was murdered. I took Barry in. Raised him like my own son. And, to my shame, I was one of the people Iris was talking about before. I was an adult, someone in a position of respect and authority, and I spent years telling Barry that his father had murdered his mother.

"I've never been happier to be wrong about something. Or more ashamed at having taken so long to believe in someone.

"I believe in Barry Allen. In his goodness. In his mind. In his commitment. I've been a cop my whole adult life. I've taken down a door or two with some of you on this panel. We've seen some things together, haven't we? I've put my faith and trust in you, and you've done the same with me.

"Believe me now: Barry Allen is a good cop. He's an essential cop.

"Is he often late? Does he forget to call? Does he space out and disappear for hours on end? Hell, I'm not gonna pretend none of that's true! I'm not even gonna pretend it doesn't drive me up a wall—it does! The kid can be a ghost sometimes.

"But he's a ghost who produces results. A ghost who has solved innumerable cases that any other CSI would've given up on. I'm sure they would have punched the clock on time and picked up the lab phone on the first ring, but does any of that matter if they don't get the job done?

"Barry Allen gets the job done. Every time. All the time. And we'd be damn fools to kick him out of this department.

"That's all I've got."

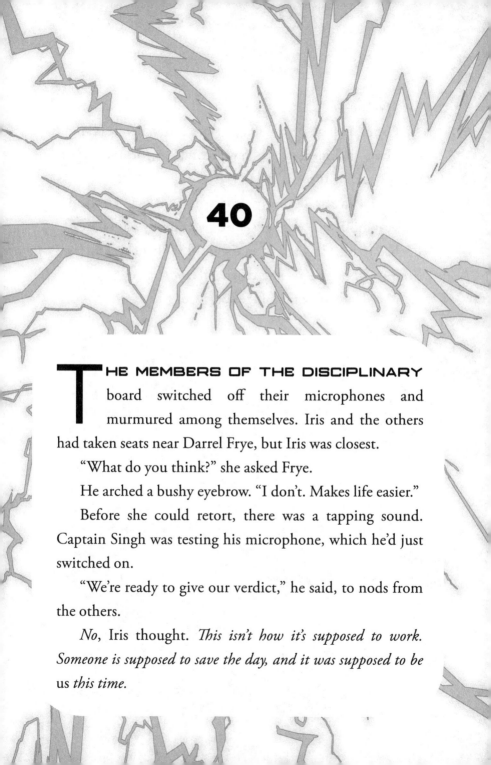

40

THE MEMBERS OF THE DISCIPLINARY board switched off their microphones and murmured among themselves. Iris and the others had taken seats near Darrel Frye, but Iris was closest.

"What do you think?" she asked Frye.

He arched a bushy eyebrow. "I don't. Makes life easier."

Before she could retort, there was a tapping sound. Captain Singh was testing his microphone, which he'd just switched on.

"We're ready to give our verdict," he said, to nods from the others.

No, Iris thought. *This isn't how it's supposed to work. Someone is supposed to save the day, and it was supposed to be us this time.*

"We are—"

Captain Singh broke off and stared straight ahead, right over Iris's shoulder. After a few seconds, it got uncomfortable. Everyone turned. Even Frye.

There, in the doorway, stood Barry Allen. He held a folder in his hand, and he seemed just slightly out of breath. Iris had to bite down *hard* on the inside of her cheek to keep from screaming in joy and relief and love.

"Am I late for something?" Barry joked.

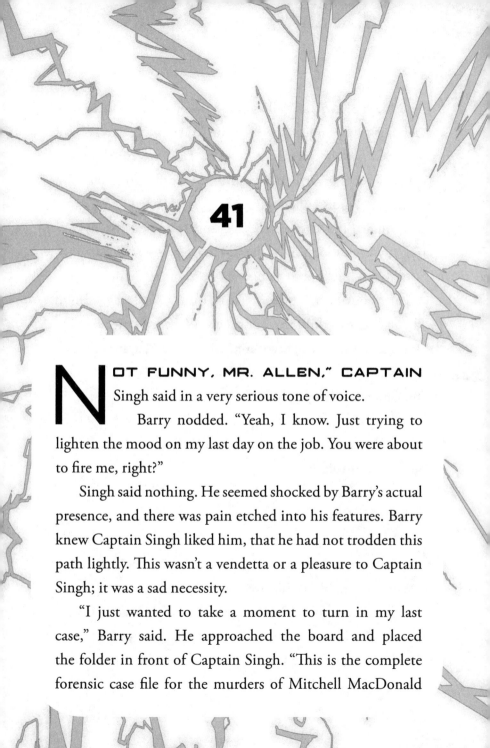

41

"NOT FUNNY, MR. ALLEN," CAPTAIN Singh said in a very serious tone of voice.

Barry nodded. "Yeah, I know. Just trying to lighten the mood on my last day on the job. You were about to fire me, right?"

Singh said nothing. He seemed shocked by Barry's actual presence, and there was pain etched into his features. Barry knew Captain Singh liked him, that he had not trodden this path lightly. This wasn't a vendetta or a pleasure to Captain Singh; it was a sad necessity.

"I just wanted to take a moment to turn in my last case," Barry said. He approached the board and placed the folder in front of Captain Singh. "This is the complete forensic case file for the murders of Mitchell MacDonald and Herb Shawn, as well as over a dozen others we can now conclusively connect to the same killer. With the help of the CCPD's contractors at S.T.A.R. Labs, I was able to put together enough evidence for the D.A.'s office to convict Dr. Herbert Hynde, a metahuman."

Singh flipped open the file and thumbed through its pages without looking at them. His eyes never left Barry.

"I was lucky and happened to see the Flash running a patrol out on the street," Barry went on. "I flagged him down and gave him the information I had. Right now, Dr. Hynde is in a special cryogenic cell at Iron Heights to stabilize him while he awaits trial." Barry licked his lips. The next bit came out shaky at first:

"Captain. Members of the disciplinary board. It's been my honor and my privilege to serve with you. I am ready to accept your ruling."

With that, he stepped back and stood next to Darrel Frye, who looked as though someone had just hit him on the head with a rubber mallet.

"Come on!" It was Joe, rising to his feet behind Barry. "Captain Singh! David. Are you really gonna do this? Look at what you've got in front of you. You put Barry on suspension a week ago, but he kept working the case. And he closed it! He took a killer off the streets after being sent to his room. No one else would have done that. And no one else would have solved it but Barry Allen. Are you really going to throw that away?"

The other two members of the disciplinary board looked over at Captain Singh, who was still staring at Barry, his jaw locked and jutting out. He strummed his fingers on the folder before him.

It seemed as though agonizing hours passed, but it was only a few seconds before Singh leaned into his microphone, cleared his throat, and said, "If it pleases the members of the board, I am going to revoke my complaint against Mr. Allen."

Barry couldn't believe it. It took a moment for everyone else to realize what had just happened. Iris reached out and took Barry's hand and squeezed it. Hard. H.R. hooted in joy, jumping up from his seat and slamming his drumsticks on the seat back before him. Cisco grabbed H.R. and shoved him back into his seat, shushing him at the same time. Barry thought he heard Joe whisper, "Yes!" Wally fist-pumped.

"Mr. Allen," Captain Singh said, very seriously, "everyone here has spoken quite eloquently and truthfully about your dedication, your skill, and your personal integrity. I'm going to say—on the record—that they are all right. And I'm also going to tell you—again, on the record—do not make me regret this decision."

"I won't let you down, sir." Barry squeezed Iris's hand back.

"Then we're adjourned," Singh said. "West. Allen. Get back to work."

As soon as the members of the board stood to leave, the members of Team Flash finally let loose, shouting and cheering and applauding. Iris stood up and threw her arms around Barry, clutching him tightly. Cisco hooted and clapped, joined by an enthusiastic Wally. Caitlin leaned in to kiss Barry's cheek. Joe slapped him on the shoulder, beaming broadly.

"You did it," he told Barry.

Darrel Frye packed up his briefcase and headed for the door. Before he left, though, he turned to Barry.

"Kid," he said, "with the kind of luck you've got, head down to the track right now and put some money on the ponies."

"It's not luck," Barry told him.

"If you tell me it's family," Frye grumbled, "I'm gonna puke."

Borne high on a wave of the love of his friends, Barry could only smile. "Grab a bucket."

Frye grunted and rolled his eyes.

Barry understood the man's cynicism. He understood it well, and once he might even have shared in it. But he'd been to the future—two of them, in fact—and he'd seen that humanity survived.

Actually, that was wrong. Humanity would not merely survive—it would thrive. He could countenance no cynicism in the face of what he'd witnessed.

And while he was certain that there were dark periods in between the two points of light he'd visited, those points of light were important markers for him, proof that what he and his friends did and cared about and accomplished mattered. Even if those futures were alternate timelines or merely possible futures, well . . . at least they were possible.

So, yes, it was family. And it was friends. And it was belief in truth, in science, in society, and in everyone around him.

Iris kissed him. "You did it," she whispered in his ear.

"*We* did it," he told her.

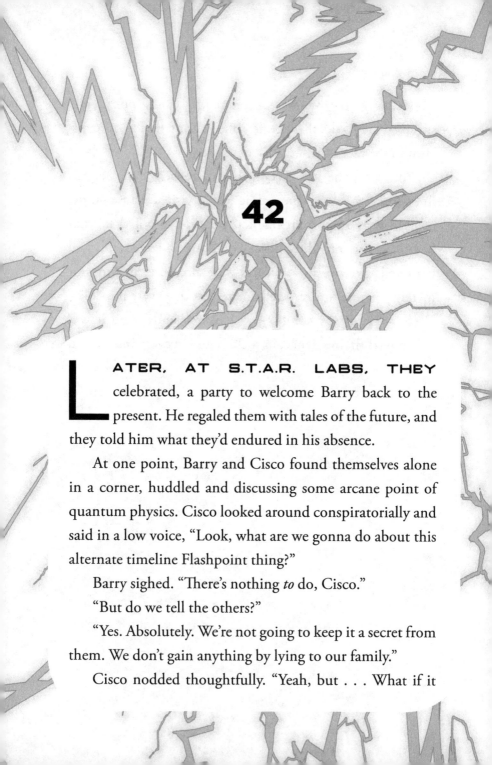

42

LATER, AT S.T.A.R. LABS, THEY celebrated, a party to welcome Barry back to the present. He regaled them with tales of the future, and they told him what they'd endured in his absence.

At one point, Barry and Cisco found themselves alone in a corner, huddled and discussing some arcane point of quantum physics. Cisco looked around conspiratorially and said in a low voice, "Look, what are we gonna do about this alternate timeline Flashpoint thing?"

Barry sighed. "There's nothing *to* do, Cisco."

"But do we tell the others?"

"Yes. Absolutely. We're not going to keep it a secret from them. We don't gain anything by lying to our family."

Cisco nodded thoughtfully. "Yeah, but . . . What if it

shakes them up? Like, *to the core* shakes them up? It's one thing knowing there's an Earth 2 doppelgänger out there. It's another knowing that there's literally another *you* out there. A *you* who's one decision away from *being* you. I mean, are we even really here? Are we just living in a cast-off version of the other timeline?"

Barry grinned. "C'mon, Cisco: It doesn't matter where we are or when we are. What matters is *who* we are. And what we do."

Cisco furrowed his brow, absorbing that. Then his face split into an enormous smile. "Yeah. Yeah, that's legit."

Just then, an alarm sounded. Barry flipped open his ring; his costume expanded out into its full size, and he had slipped it on by the time Cisco had rushed to his computer and flung himself into his chair.

"Metahuman alert!" Cisco shouted. "Looks like we've got an old-fashioned super-villain team-up in progress, guys and gals. Weather Wizard and Rainbow Raider are robbing the First Bank of Central City on Novick Street!"

Barry turned to Wally, who had already donned his Kid Flash costume. "You up for it?"

A grin. "I was born up for it!"

They fist-bumped, and then they ran, and then they won.

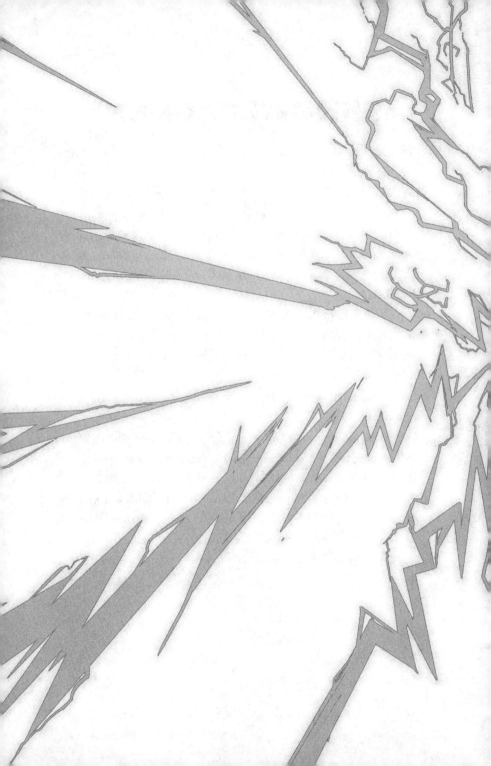

ACKNOWLEDGMENTS

I'M SO THRILLED THAT I HAD THE CHANCE to bring this story to you. And it wouldn't have been possible without the fine folks at ABRAMS and The CW/Warner Bros.

First up, the crew at Warner Bros. and The CW: Thank you so much to Greg Berlanti, Todd Helbing, Sarah Schechter, Carl Ogawa, Lindsay Kiesel, Janice Aguilar-Herrero, Catherine Shin, Thomas Zellers, Kristin Chin, Amy Weingartner, and Josh Anderson for letting me play with their toys.

Also thanks to the ABRAMS gang: Pam Bobowicz, Melanie Chang, Andrew Smith, Maggie Lehrman, Chad Beckerman, Evangelos Vasilakis, Alison Gervais, Maya Bradford, Hallie Patterson, and Liz Fithian for making this dream possible.

César Moreno once again brought the thunder and lightning with a terrific cover.

And a special thanks to my wife and my children, loves of my life, for understanding why I had to close the door to my office so many times. It's worth it—my three-year-old knows the Flash on sight!

Finally, my deepest gratitude to the legion of comic book artists, writers, and editors who have guided Barry Allen's adventures since those early days. You thrilled me as a child and inspired me as an adult. The Flash gets to run into the future, and thanks to you, we get to go with him.

ABOUT THE AUTHOR

BARRY LYGA is the author of the *New York Times* bestselling I Hunt Killers series and many other critically acclaimed middle-grade and young adult novels. A self-proclaimed Flash fanatic, Barry lives and podcasts near New York City with his family. Find him online at barrylyga.com.

253

A new criminal mastermind has descended upon Central City—one who can manipulate reality and control the actions of others. With a flick of his wand, the evil Hocus Pocus can make his audience laugh . . . he can make them applaud . . . he can even make them do his bidding.

But how?

When the Flash falls under Hocus Pocus's spell, it's up to the superspeedster—along with the help of Team Flash—to solve the mystery before he's forced to do the unthinkable!

Team Flash is still reeling from the chaos wrought by Hocus Pocus. His magic was mind-boggling but his disappearance even more so. There's only one way to conquer his madness: figure out how it all began.

The Flash plans to travel to Earth 2, but instead he lands in a world where everything is the exact opposite of what he knows. Including the villain in this town. Johnny Quick looks like the Flash. He runs like the Flash. He . . . may be the Flash?

But the only way for the real Flash to get home is to beat this superspeedster at his own game.

SOAR INTO ACTION
WITH SUPERGIRL!

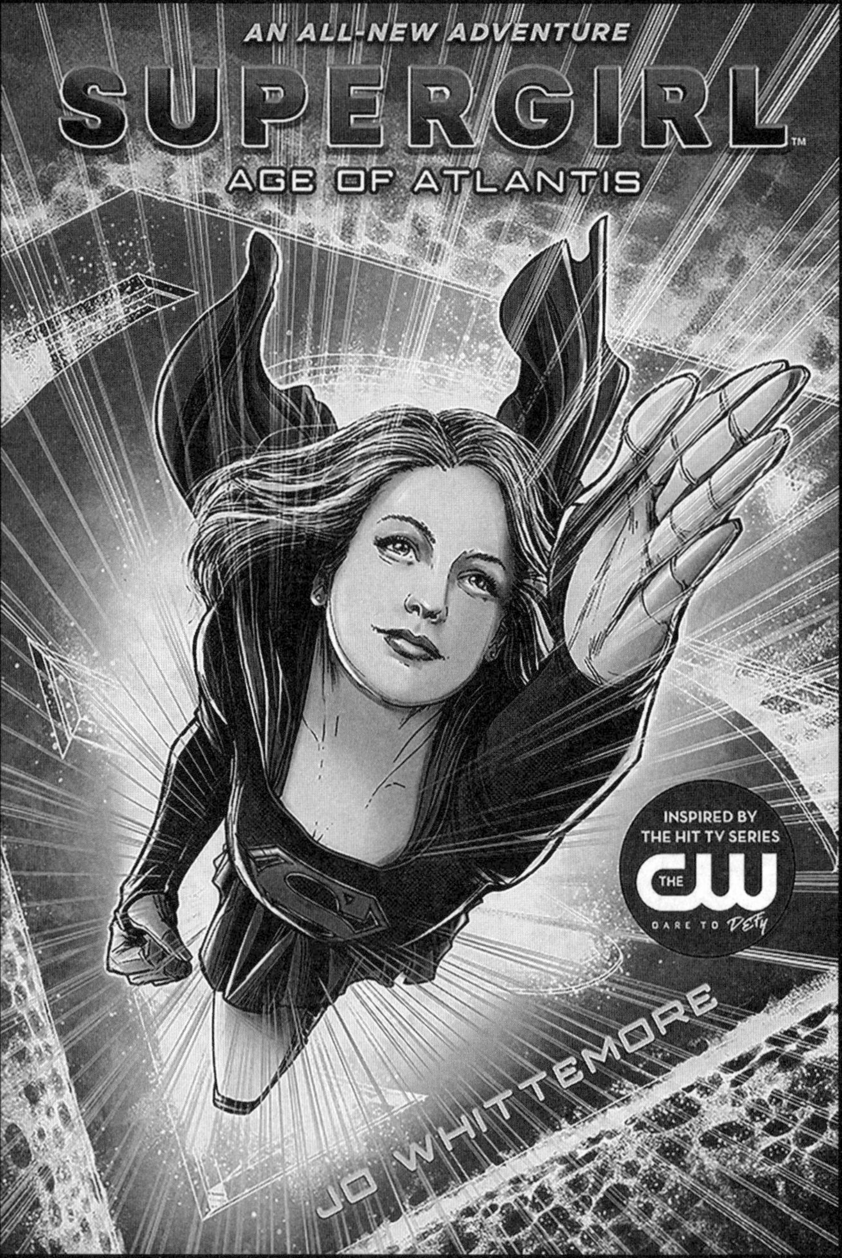

All over National City, ordinary citizens have been perform-ing amazing—and dangerous—feats. As if that wasn't weird enough, the Department of Extranormal Operations has cap-tured a humanoid sea creature on a mysterious mission.

Could these incidents be related? Supergirl must discover the connection between the furious sea creature and the recent surge of supercitizens before they cause any more damage to the city—or worse, to themselves!

DON'T MISS THE ACTION-PACKED SECOND BOOK!

AN ALL-NEW ADVENTURE

SUPERGIRL

CURSE OF THE ANCIENTS

INSPIRED BY
THE HIT TV SERIES

THE CW

DARE TO DEFY

JO WHITTEMORE

National City has recovered from an influx of supercitizens wielding their new powers against each other, and Kara Danvers is hoping for a few weeks of calm in order to focus on her career. She may secretly be a superhero, but she's surrounded by super friends whose achievements are breathtaking.

But when Caesar's Comet comes into view, a powerful curse is unleashed on National City, turning it into Ancient Rome. Supergirl and the DEO have five days to figure out who cast the curse and to reverse it. Otherwise, National City may be stuck in the past forever.